WAYNE'S DEAD

by

Christy Tillery French

AmErica House
Baltimore

First printing

ISBN: 1-59129-197-6
PUBLISHED BY AMERICA HOUSE BOOK PUBLISHERS
www.publishamerica.com
Baltimore

Printed in the United States of America

~ Dedication ~

For Cyndi,
my sister not only in the familial
sense but also in spirit,
who walks in sunshine.

For my dear friend
Theresa. Thanks for
your continued encouragement
and support. I love
you, girlfriend.

Charity
9/31/03

~ Acknowledgements ~

The author wishes to thank the following people: Arthur Bohanan, forensic expert, formerly with the Knoxville Police Department, for his professional input and patience in taking the time to answer my many questions; my sister, Cyndi Hodges, for her invaluable help in editing and critiquing, and for sharing this dream with me; my friend, author Evelyn Horan, for her much-appreciated advice and support; my good friend, author Victoria Taylor Murray, for her generous guidance as I've traveled this road of authorship along with her continual words of encouragement; my son, Jonathan, and my daughter, Meghann, for their creativity and input; and my husband, Steve, for his patience with the camera.

PROLOGUE

The small child hovers in a corner of the room in the dark, her knees drawn up to her chest, her face covered by her hands, trembling, tears running down her face.

"Please, don't let him hurt me; please, don't let him hurt me; please, don't let him hurt me," she prays to no one, to anyone. She hears his heavy tread on the steps, begins shaking her head violently side to side, whispering, "No, no, no," over and over again. Then sobbing softly, wondering why her mother doesn't stop him. Doesn't she hear, doesn't she know what he is doing to her? She has to, has to.

The door opens slowly. Already her lower body is throbbing as if in great pain. It is bad enough the damage he does to her with his belt, but what he does afterwards with his hands and body is unthinkable, pure torture.

"Please," she whimpers as he stands in the doorway, silhouetted by the light from the hallway behind him. He looks to be a giant standing there, glaring at her. She imagines his eyes are red, like a demon's. She hates him for the torture she endures at his hands. She hates everyone else for letting him do it.

He switches on the lights, advancing in the room, closing the door behind him. He stands there, watching her, a sardonic smile on his face, seeming pleased by her great fear of him.

"Come here to me," he says, his voice mild, stopping his advance when he comes to her bed.

She seems frozen, except for her ragged breathing and the tears running down her cheeks.

He reaches down, unbuckles his belt, shucks it out of his pants. She covers her eyes.

"I said, come here to me, you little bitch," he snarls, doubling the belt, snapping it.

She jumps as if startled. Then slowly, her back against the wall, she stands, but her feet won't move, refusing to carry her to the ordeal she knows is coming.

"I better not have to come over there and get you, girl," he says,

5

his voice mild once more.

Her face transgresses, becoming stony, rigid. Her eyes, glinting like algae-ridden ice, glare with hatred as she wipes her nose with the back of one hand, then begins walking toward him. Her tears are gone. When she gets to him, before he put his hands on her, she says, "My name's Ronnie, not girl."

CHAPTER 1
(ATLANTA, GEORGIA - 10 YEARS LATER)

The couple lay on the bed, oblivious to the activity going on around them.

On each nightstand is a lone glass, showing a small amount of liquor laced with a strong sedative, which they had been unaware of as they had laid in bed, as they did every night, drinking a small brandy before bedtime.

Their daughter is using the remaining liquor to pour over their supine bodies. When she is finished, she places the empty bottle on the bed, as if it has fallen over, spilling its contents, then pulls out a drawer in her father's nightstand, fishes out a pack of Marlboros and a butane lighter, shakes out a lone cigarette, then neatly puts the pack back where she had gotten it, being careful to close the drawer.

She steps back from her parents, looking at them, watching, wishing there had been some way her father could have been awake for his death that would not be detected when the arson investigator starts snooping around. Finally, sighing dejectedly, knowing time is running out, she brings the butane lighter up to the cigarette and lights it.

She takes a deep drag, then holds the cigarette away from her, watching its glowing end.

She retrieves her mother's glass, holds it up in the air as if in a toast, and says, "Here's to you, Daddy, may you burn in hell forever for what you've done to your little girl, and Mama right along with you, for letting you do it," turns the glass, drains the contents over the bed, wipes her fingerprints off with the tail of her shirt, then throws it on the bed. She does the same with her father's glass, then lays the cigarette on the alcohol-soaked sheet covering her father's body. Watches a small flame flare, then sputter, then flare again. Waits as the flame ignites the alcohol, burning a trail up toward her father's face.

Stays as long as she dares, watching the flames licking almost lovingly at her parents' bodies, thinking, *burn, damn you, burn.*

Feeling the heat as the flames intensify, noting they have moved to the curtains covering the window behind the bed, she pockets the butane lighter and silently leaves the room, making sure to close the door quietly behind her.

CHAPTER 2
(ASHEVILLE, NORTH CAROLINA - 1995)

The matronly, somewhat elderly woman slowly traversed the carpeted hallway, her rubber-soled shoes emitting whispery noises, the cart she was pushing occasionally giving out a rather startled squeak as if running over a small animal, finally stopping at the door at the end of the hallway. She did what she had always done, what she had been instructed to do, gave two sharp raps to the hotel room door, to ascertain if anyone was still there, even though check-out time was two hours past.

If someone had answered, she would have simply asked if they were ready for her to clean, but since no one responded to her knocks, she inserted her master key into the lock and let herself in.

She stood inside the entryway, letting the light from the hallway into the darkened room, feeling the hairs on the nape of her neck rise, for no apparent reason.

Well, danged if somebody didn't just walk over my grave, she thought ironically, tugging her cleaning cart in, letting the door close behind it as she pulled her cart into the sitting area.

She stood, observing the room, taking note nothing really looked out of place, her eyes then landing on a coat thrown across the chair by the reading lamp, then darting to the door leading to the bedroom, which was closed.

"'Scuse me," she called out, "is anyone here?"

Again, she felt her hackles rise.

She rubbed the goose bumps on her arms, thinking without knowing the word that it seemed preternaturally quiet in here. No, that was wrong. Unnaturally still, void maybe.

She approached the closed door with trepidation, stood there, not wanting to open it.

What the hell's wrong with you, Maggie? she mentally asked herself, irritated at her apprehension over nothing. *Just open the durn door, change the sheets on the bed, empty the garbage cans, clean the bathroom, then get the hell out of Dodge. You done this same job a hundred thousand times or more, so what's got into you today?*

She cautiously put her hand on the door, gave it a light push. It creaked open, sounding like something out of a horror movie. She jumped a little at the squeak, then laughed harshly at herself.

"Anybody in here?" she called loudly, exasperated with her behavior.

Angry with herself, she shoved open the door, noticed the dimness save for the bar of light spilling into the room from where the curtains had parted, her eyes finding a lumpish form on the bed. There was a bad smell coming from that room, one which she couldn't quite process.

"Oh, I'm sorry," she said, embarrassed. "I didn't think anyone was in . . . ."

But there was something odd about that form, something that didn't fit right with her mind.

She took a tentative step into the room, thinking, *Oh, God, don't be some old geyser who went and had himself a heart attack, please don't. If he is, you ain't gonna scream, Maggie,* she chided herself. *You got more balls than to stand there screaming like some little helpless dingbat, like one of those young airheads your employer is so fond of hiring.*

"Hello?" she asked and waited. She had never noticed how awfully quiet it was in these rooms.

"You there on the bed, you all right?" she called.

The form did not stir.

She considered opening the drapes for more light but instead went closer to the bed, froze when her eyes processed it as a nude man, sprawled on his back. His face was contorted into a grimace of either pure pain or pure ecstacy, she couldn't tell which. *He has to be dead, for sure, looking like that,* she thought. She closed her eyes for a moment, fighting for control, then turned away and opened them and was staring at his body. There was some really dark liquid on him down there, a lot of it, she noticed, her face reddening at seeing his exposed genitals. There was less of the same dark stuff on his chest, but not much. None on his face. *Surely that ain't blood,* she thought. *Nah, probably that scented sex oil stuff the younger girls talked about.* She wrinkled her nose at the coppery smell, refusing to entertain the thought of what actually might be on the man's body.

Her eyes traveled around the bed, then over. There were large letters scrawled in great big, spindly shapes on the wall above the bed, dark ribbons running down, leaving trails as if a pack of bloody snails had traveled through. *Surely that ain't blood,* she thought again; but the smell, she felt like she was going to gag, it was so strong.

"Does that say somethin'?" she whispered to herself. She went to the curtains, pulled them open, letting light into the room, then stood studying the wall. "W-A -- is that Wayne -- Wayne's? Wayne's what? Rear?" she asked, glanced at the man, then back to the letters. Her mouth opened. "Dead?" she asked aloud. "Wayne's Dead?" she said, looking at him.

"Mister?" she asked, "you all right?" mentally kicking herself, telling herself he was not all right, *Look at his face, for God's sake, Maggie, you stupid shit! Ain't no doubt that man won't be getting up and walking out of here.*

Without realizing it, she advanced toward the bed, fascinated with the expression on his face, thinking ironically that's how her Joe always looked right when he would . . . .

"Damned if he didn't go and have a heart attack," she said out loud, feeling proud she hadn't once felt the inclination to scream, not even with whatever smelly trash was on the body and used for that eerie writing above the bed, then turning around, intending to go call for help, felt something slick and squishy beneath her foot. She stopped, looked down, then bent over and peered more closely, not understanding what was on the floor.

She straightened up, looked at the body, then back at the wall, opened her mouth, screamed for all she was worth, screamed until her nausea drove her into the bathroom, opened her mouth once more, and threw up.

CHAPTER 3
(KNOXVILLE, TN - PRESENT DAY)

They were known as the M&M boys, or the Pres brothers, depending on who was doing the calling. The reason being that their names were James Madison and James Monroe respectively (both named for the presidents, don't you know). Their nicknames were Jimmy and you couldn't distinguish one from the other by calling him Jimmy M. As for using monikers, the two looked so much alike, it was hard to tell which one you were speaking to. One was a month older than the other, but you couldn't tell that from looking at them. They might have been identical twins, for all anyone knew. It was suspicioned within the department that they were actually brothers, although it was known their mothers were different. However, seeing as how their respective matriarchs lived in the projects near each other and one certain gentleman had been known to visit both from time to time, and seeing as how these two young officers looked so much alike and were about as thick as any two men could be, what else was there to think? Thus, the aforementioned M&M boys and Pres brothers referrals evolved.

These two were rookie cops who had been on the force just long enough to make a name for themselves. They had grown up in the projects, vowing to themselves and each other time after time that if they survived to adulthood, they were gonna become policemen and do some kind of damage to the drug dealers that hung around that area. They were the only officers ever who had volunteered to be placed on one of the most dangerous beats in Knoxville. That got them some sort of respect, right off. Well, other than those that opined these two were crazy, in a disrespectful sort of way, but they didn't count.

The Pres boys were big men and could be some mean M-fer's. They went into that project and were doing their own kind of damage, kicking ass and making headway in their own war against drugs. Dealing was still accomplished; however, much more covertly than in the olden days. As for their tendency to be physically violent with certain unsavory characters, the department turned its somewhat biased eye the other way. They didn't want to know anything about it. These two big, bad policemen didn't know it, but they were about to come upon a sight that would stay with them the rest of their days.

They were headed on their usual cruise, going from the downtown station out to their particular area, when the call came over the radio from dispatch. They looked at each other, both with wide grins on their faces. The passenger M&M picked up the radio, called in they were headed that direction and would handle the call.

They drove to a swank hotel on the outskirts of downtown Knoxville, importantly strode into the lobby, and after being directed to the top floor by a reservations clerk, found a pale-looking security guard waiting for them. His first words to them should have warned them what was coming. "Man, I hope you didn't have no breakfast," he said, heading down the hallway. They looked at each other, not grinning this time, then followed along behind, both thinking, *Sheeiitt, what a weenie.*

That attitude changed as soon as the guard opened the door to a suite on the top floor, indicating with a sweep of his hand the open door to the bedroom, where they could see a nude man sprawled on the bed on his back. There was blood everywhere. The smell of death was incredible. Both men hovered back, as if afraid to cross over the threshold, not so sure they wanted to handle this now.

The security guard stepped inside the suite, breathing through his mouth, then turned to face them, waiting. Seeing they didn't look to be in any kind of hurry to follow, he rolled his eyes, then said, "One of you's got to determine if this guy is dead or what, so we'll know who to call," then watched as two Adam's apples bobbed nervously up and down.

"Why ain't you done that?" the older M&M asked, sidling closer to the bedroom, staring in awe at the blood splattered on the wall behind the bed.

"Hell, ain't my job," the security guard said, giving a nervous glance at the body. "Just get on in there and let's see if this dude's dead or what. I been told that's the proper protocol."

"Well, looks pretty obvious to me, he's dead," the younger M&M said, standing close to his partner. "Shit, look at all that blood. Nobody could still be alive, losing that much blood."

His eyes traveled to the wall behind the bed, where large, red, spindly letters had been written in what looked like runny raspberry jello. He pointed, said, "Hey, what's that say? Is that W-A-G --"

"No, man, that's W-A-Y, what?" the older policeman said.

"Wayne," the security guard said, studying the wall. "It says Wayne - Wayne's Dead."

"That the guy's name?" the older Pres brother asked.

"How the hell you expect me to know?" the security guard asked angrily. "Now, come on, do what you're supposed to do, what you were trained to do. We got to get moving here before word gets out all over the hotel and then we got mass chaos, not to mention the media standing around interviewing everybody and their brother."

"Look, the proper protocol is, we see a dead body, we don't go anywhere near it, we call dispatch for the special investigations unit," the older M&M said.

"Do you know for a fact that guy's dead?" the security guard asked with irritation.

"Well, no," he answered. "But I don't see how he can be alive, all that . . ."

"Just do your job, man," the security guard said, "so we can deal with this problem, all right?"

The brothers looked at each other. An exchange of words seemed to go on with their eyes. Finally, the older one sighed, said, "Awright, already," irritably and stepped into the room. Approaching the bed more closely, he began to gag at the rich, coppery smell. Placing his hand over his nose, he felt something slippery give beneath his feet, looked down, wasn't sure what he was stepping on, so bent over and peered closer. He glanced at the body, then down again. Finally realizing what the object of review was, he inaudibly mumbled a rather crude epitaph, put his hand over his mouth, and went toward the door, making gagging noises, barely stepping into the hallway before he lost anything and everything that was in his stomach.

His younger partner watched with concern, fighting his own gagging impulse, then smelling the acrid stench of vomit superimposed on the bitter smell of blood, pulled out a handkerchief, placed it over his face, stepped into the room, approached the corpse, sidestepping whatever the hell had gotten to his partner, took one look, quickly backed out, mumbled toward the security guard, "I got to call this in, that guy's as dead as dead can get," then went further down the hall to get away from all the stench, fighting the need to vomit all the way.

CHAPTER 4

There was an incessant buzzing sound coming from far away but seeming to grow louder with each audible perception. He stuffed a pillow over his head, snuggled deeper under the covers, trying to get away, trying to get back to where he had been. He felt a sharp jab in his ribs, jumped at that, followed by an even stronger one.

"Dammit, Beth, that hurt," he growled, throwing the pillow at the buried form next to him, reaching out, picking up the receiver of the phone.

"Daniels," he said, trying to sound wide-awake, listened for a minute, then, "On my way," hanging up the phone.

"I just remembered why I could not tolerate being married to a cop," he heard his ex-wife's muffled voice say.

He sighed, closed his eyes, thinking, *Let's not get into that!*

The bed shook slightly as she rolled over against him. He felt her tongue licking the tender area her elbow had earlier assaulted, then her hand sliding down his trunk.

"Don't start what won't get finished," he groused.

"Says who," she murmured, her tongue following her hand. He moaned lowly, feeling liquid fire stroking his tumescence.

"Bethany," he said, warningly.

"Hmmmm?" she answered, quickly working her tongue. He sighed, then with reluctance, gently pushed her away.

"Come on, Jack, just a quickie, you can at least give me that, can't you?" poking her head out from underneath the covers.

"No can do," he said, his voice brusque, sitting up, throwing his legs over the side of the bed.

"You jerk!" she complained irritably.

He took the time to look at her. "Geez, Bethany, that's a really profound observation, coming from a psychiatrist."

She sneered.

He stared at her, his beauty of an ex-wife, all black and white interspersed here and there with pink: raven-dark hair, coal-black eyes, thick ebony eyelashes matched by dark eyebrows, pale, milky complexion, pale strawberry lips, creamy, voluptuous breasts tippled mauve-pink, long pale trunk and legs interrupted at their juncture with that thick, black pelt. He remembered what a turn-on that used to be for him and wondered exactly when and why he fell out of love with her. Wondered why he still slept with her, when he really couldn't stand her, to be honest about it. Wondered why the sex was still so good.

Turning his back on her, he began to dress, forcing his thoughts from the erstwhile to the present.

Heard her sigh heavily. Ignored her.

"You really are a jerk," she said.

Felt himself bristle at the whining tone of her voice. He thought, *Yeah, that's one of the reasons I fell out of love with her.* He turned to face her, taking note she was favoring him with her sullen look. Thought, *That's another reason I fell out of love with her,* as he said, "That call was about a homicide at the Hyatt, Bethany. Whether you like it or not, I am a detective, and as a detective, it is part of my job to investigate homicides, even when it might interfere with your precious plans. How hard can it be to understand that?"

She gave him a coy look. "What's wrong, Jack, don't I turn you on anymore?"

"You have to ask me that after last night?" he asked, zipping his pants, pulling his shirt on.

A secretive smile crossed her lips. This irritated him.

"You never did tell me what you wanted," he said, buttoning his shirt, staring at her bared breasts above the covers, irritated at himself for letting her seduce him once more.

She shrugged. "It wasn't really important," looking at him with those smoldering eyes.

They stared at each other for a moment. "Listen, Beth, this needs to stop," Jack finally said, surprised he picked that moment to bring the subject up.

She gave him an innocent look. "What does?"

"This continuing to fu – see each other," he snapped, watching her face form another pout. "Now, don't get mad, but you have to realize this isn't good for us, still screw – "

"It's called making love, Jack," she said in an angry tone, sitting up, causing her breasts to move prettily.

He sighed this time. "Listen, Beth, what I'm trying to say is, we're divorced now. We need to get on with our lives, our separate lives. Surely you can understand that."

Her eyes narrowed, her pale face flushed. *Black and white, dappled with pink*, he couldn't help thinking.

"Don't take this the wrong way, Bethany. You're a psychiatrist, you ought to understand what I'm saying. We need to close out what we had – "

"You should have been an accountant, the way you talk," she flung at him, throwing the covers away, getting up.

He shook his head disparagingly, knowing there was no use talking to her when she got like this, turned his back on her. Wondered for the millionth time how someone as screwed up as his ex-wife could counsel people who were also supposedly screwed up. *The blind leading the blind, I guess*, he thought.

He heard her angry movements as she put her clothes on, then feeling guilty, turned around, said, "Beth, I'm sorry. It's just, this can't be good for the two of us. We're not moving forward, not going on, we're still at the same place we were when we divorced."

"Then why the fuck do you still fuck me?" she screamed in his face.

"You're the one who came to me," he yelled back.

"To talk to you, Jack, simply to talk. You started it, you always do."

He stared at her, flabbergasted. Hadn't she been the one who had kissed him passionately, who had begun removing his clothes? But he had responded to her, he had made love to her, he had to admit that.

He nodded his head and said, "I've got to go, Beth, I really don't have time to get into this now."

"And how many times have I heard that line?" she ranted.

He snatched his keys off the nightstand. "I'll talk to you later. You can let yourself out," he called over his shoulder as he headed out.

"That's right, Jack, run away like you always do," she yelled after him. "Don't stand up and face whatever the problem is, just go on out that door, why don't – "

He slammed the door, cutting her off. "And how many times have I heard that line?" he said softly to himself.

CHAPTER 5

He strode into the Hyatt, a tall man with an athletic build, wide shoulders, narrow hips, long legs. He seemed unaware of the interest generated his way by both men and women: he was used to it. With the male sector, it was the badge he wore clipped to his belt, the air of authority which seemed to hover around him. With the female gender, it was more a physical aspect. He was a good-looking man in a rugged sort of way with dark eyes under heavy black eyebrows, dark-brown hair which tended to curl as it lengthened. His mouth was narrow, his nose long and straight. He usually carried a mean expression on his face, one he had cultivated. This was what women found most appealing about him.

His investigative partner was waiting on him by the elevators. The only indication Jack gave he even saw the guy was a slight nod of the head as they stepped onto the elevator together.

As they rode up, Marvin studied him, then said, "You in a blue mood or just mad about somethin'?"

Jack glanced his way, gave him a slight frown, then shook his head as if in despair.

"Lord, God, don't tell me you been at it with your ex again," Marvin said, acting disgusted.

Jack couldn't stop one corner of his mouth from turning up.

"When you gonna learn, fool?" Marvin fussed. "That girl ain't got nothing you want, least nothing you can't get from somebody else."

Jack shrugged noncommittally.

"Or does she?" Marvin asked, acting interested.

Jack let a snort escape.

"Hear it's bad up there," Marvin said, casting eyes upwards.

"Yeah?" Jack asked, turning to him.

"Security guard said there's blood everywhere. Said the smell is something else, fer sure."

Jack nodded. He was used to this.

"Said it ain't your typical killing, though. Indicated there's a surprise waiting on us."

Jack lifted his eyebrows, nodded his head as the elevator stopped, then stepped off.

They were immediately met by what looked to be a gang of policemen who were lined along the hallway, standing around, talking, trying to act important.

"Word's out, I guess," Marvin mumbled, then raising his voice, "Any of you cadets ain't got any business here, I would advise you to vacate the premises. The posse has arrived."

There was a lot of grinning, good-natured protests. No one made a move to leave, all eyes following the two investigators.

Jack stopped outside the room, looking around. *God, the blood smell was terrible even out here, made worse by the stench of vomit.* He noticed a towel on the carpet in front of his feet. "What's that and who the hell threw up?"

One of the rookies ambled over. "One of the M&M boys upchucked," he said, grinning. "Don't step on that towel, 'cause that's where it happened."

Jack pulled out Vicks salve, applied some under his nose, turning to watch the EMS team, which was approaching.

"I reckon you got the honors on this one," one of the paramedics said, giving him a grimace.

Jack glanced at his watch, then looked at Marvin.

"Crime scene specialists are on their way, should be here any minute," Marvin answered his unspoken question.

"Who answered the call?"

"The M&M boys," Marvin said, looking around, then waving one over. *The older one,* Jack thought.

"You caught it?" Jack asked.

"Yeah, man, sure wish we hadn't, though," he said, glancing into the room, then away.

"That bad, huh?" Marvin asked.

"Whatchoo think, man, all that blood on the wall?" the officer said, looking around for his partner.

"You secured the room?" Jack asked.

"Yeah, yeah, we done that, all right," he answered.

Marvin glanced into the room, then back at the cop. "Anybody go in there, touch anything?"

Their answer was a sheepish look.

"Shit, man, you know better than that," Marvin said, his voice

20

chiding.

The older policeman shifted restlessly. "The security guard wouldn't confirm the dude was dead, said I had to do that."

Jack frowned. "You know the procedure is for any death, our unit gets called."

"Well, yeah, but the security guard thought maybe the guy was still alive. Told me to make sure one way or the other. That's when we called you guys, after we seen the dude was dead."

"So what'd you disturb?" Marvin asked, impatiently.

"Well, I didn't actually touch it, you see," the officer explained. "It was kind of laying on the floor and I, well, I guess I kinda stepped on it."

"Stepped on what?" Jack asked, frowning.

"The guy's left nut. Cut clean off'n the body, just laying there on the floor. I didn't see it when I went in there, all that blood and everything, 'cause I was checking on the body, you see."

"So we know any kind of shoe print left on the man's left testicle comes from you," Jack mused. "We can rule that out right off, right?"

"Well, yeah, you could say that," the young cop said.

Marvin gave Jack a wide grin.

"Okay, let's get rid of all those who don't need to be here, start asking some questions, find out who this guy is, who heard what," Jack instructed.

"I reckon his name's Wayne," the young patrolman offered. Jack and Marvin looked at him. "It says 'Wayne's Dead' up over the bed there," he explained, pointing. "Otherwise, why'd that particular name be up there?"

"One word of advice," Jack said, facing the patrolman again. "Never assume anything. Not in this line of work."

"Ain't that fer sure," Marvin agreed.

The officer just stood there.

"Move," Jack said, his voice mild.

"Yes, sir," he answered, walking quickly away, assuming an importance stance, maneuvering among the other policemen, telling them to get busy doing something.

"Who's the other investigator?" Jack asked.

"I think Robin's got this one," Marvin said, leaning against the door, watching the mask drop over Jack's face.

They heard the elevator ping, watched as the lead crime scene specialist and his two associates stepped off and walked toward them.

Jack grinned at the head specialist, who grinned back as he headed toward him. Jack really got a kick out of this guy. He stopped in front of Jack, put his hand out.

"Jackson, how you doing today?" he asked, a mischievous gleam in his eye, running his hand through his unruly gray hair.

"'Bout as good as usual, Bogie," Jack said, his smile widening. There was something about the way this guy's face was put together and his constant good humor that always put Jack in a better frame of mind.

"So, what's going on?" Bogie asked, adjusting the glasses on his face, glancing into the room.

"EMS just left, turned it over to us, so we can go on in once we strategize," Marvin answered.

"Before anybody goes in, there's a severed left testicle lying on the floor somewhere around the bed," Jack said, watching the smile erupt on Bogie's face.

"Ouch," he said in a mild tone. "Sure hope the man was dead before he lost it."

They all grinned.

"Correction," Marvin said. "Make that severed left testicle with a standard issue police boot size what, Jack, 13, maybe, on it."

"Probably squashed right into the carpet," Jack said.

"Probably obliterated with a foot that big coming down on it," Bogie said.

They all laughed.

The elevator pinged and the third investigator stepped off: Robin, a short, round woman with chestnut-colored hair and violet eyes, perky as the quintessential cheerleader. It was the goal of the majority of the men on the police force to take Robin to bed. Jack had been there, done that, and regretted it mightily.

Robin planted a bright smile on her face, acknowledging greetings from the other cops, as she headed toward the group cloistered outside the room, dreading having to work with Jack, that jerk.

Once she had joined them and all had exchanged greetings, Jack filled her in on what they knew so far.

"Okay, we'll go in first," Bogey said, waving toward his two assistants. "We'll do the graph sketch, get the pictures and video, then let's get that severed testicle into evidence before we bag anything else."

Marvin pointed toward the floor. "Make sure you don't step on that towel. One of the M&M boys got sick."

Jack watched Bogie and his assistants carefully advance into the room, take up their positions, begin their routine, then turned to Robin. "Why don't you supervise the M&M boys, get them asking people on this floor if they saw or heard anything," he told her.

She gave him a brisk nod, then turned and left.

"Man, was she sending you the evil eye," Marvin said as they headed toward the elevators.

"Who?" Jack asked, distracted.

"Robin, man. I saw the way she was looking at you, that gleam in her eyes. Shit, Jack, is there any woman on earth you can get along with?"

Jack ignored him.

"Now, if you'd listen to me 'cause I, being a connoisseur of women, know of what I speak, you'd have women falling all over themselves trying to get to you."

Jack huffed.

Marvin ignored that. "You got to learn to treat 'em with kindness, a lot of sugar, dude, not act like your namesake."

Jack rolled his eyes. "Why is it everyone has to comment on my name?" he asked no one in particular.

"Well, what's it taste like? All tart and heavy and sour. Can't treat a woman like that and expect her to like you, much less love you. Got to treat her with kindness and gentleness, show her – "

"What's the name of the security guard?" Jack asked, cutting him off, punching the elevator button.

Marvin shrugged, stepping into the open elevator. "Looks like a short, skinny Rodney Dangerfield, is all I know."

Jack turned to him, frowning. "Sometimes I have an awful time understanding how you got in the department, Marvin. What was it, guy, affirmative action?"

23

"Don't start on me, man. You know what I got to say about affirmative action," Marvin ranted. "Hell, I got where I am through my skill, my instinct, my superior intelligence to you, so don't you go questioning my investigative skills. I'll put you under the table any old day, we get into that."

Jack nodded as if to say, sure.

They found the security guard standing by the reception desk, gossiping with the reservations clerks.

At least Marvin described him accurately, Jack thought as they approached, watching the man's nervous habit of moving restlessly while standing still, shuffling his feet, jutting his chin forward, extending his neck out, just like Rodney Dangerfield. He had the same bug eyes, gray hair, and beer gut as the comedian, but with the build of Barney Fife.

Jack stopped in front of him. "Jack Daniels," he said, not offering his hand.

"Hey, just like the – "

"You want to tell us who found the body and go from there?" Jack interrupted.

"It was one of our housekeepers," the man said, pointing. "She's in the office there. You can talk to her if you want."

Jack turned and looked at Marvin, who, reading his unspoken request, went toward the office.

"She screamed loud enough to wake the dead, went running down the hall, and somebody from one of the rooms upstairs called down and reported a housekeeper on the rampage." He grinned as if thinking this was funny. Jack kept a rigid face.

"Anyway, I went upstairs, got out of her what she seen, went to the door, saw all that blood on the wall. Man, I never seen so much blood in my life, and I been around, let me tell you," glancing at Jack to see if he appreciated this. He didn't. "So, I backed on out, not wanting to disturb any evidence, and called 911. Just like I've been instructed to do," he finished defensively.

Jack nodded. "Any idea who the guy is?"

The guard puffed up. "I already looked into that," he said. "He signed in as John Wayne. I guess that's where the Wayne comes in over the bed, don't you think?"

"If that's his actual name," Jack said. "Where's the registration card?" he asked, stepping up to the reservations clerk, who promptly handed it over.

Jack turned back to the security guard, giving him a frustrated look. "Why are you letting people handle this card? There could be prints on it needed in this investigation."

The man's face went white. Jack pulled out a cellophane envelope, pushed the card off the desk with his pen into the envelope, then studied it, recognizing the address on the card as the one for the courthouse. *Shit*, he thought, *should have known this wouldn't be easy.*

"Don't go away," he said, went to a phone, called in, asked if there had been any missing persons reports filed for a middle-aged white man within the past forty-eight hours, sorry, he didn't have any other information yet. Receiving an answer in the negative, he walked toward the office, stood in the doorway, listening to the housekeeper try to explain in broken English to Marvin the terrible scene she had witnessed.

Jack went back to the reservations clerk, asked to speak to the manager. A few minutes later, a woman in her late thirties approached him and identified herself as Ms. Shafer, the manager, and Jack asked for the names, addresses, and phone numbers of all employees of the hotel on duty from ten p.m., the time of check-in for the man in room 703, to the time his body was found. She told him she would start working on that right away and quickly left.

He turned to the security guard. "What time did you come on duty last night?" he asked.

The guy shrugged restlessly. "'Bout eleven, I guess, give or take a minute."

"You see or hear anything suspicious?" Jack asked, giving him his most intense stare.

He thought importantly, then, unsettled by Jack's look, said, "Uh, no, nothing. It was a quiet night."

"No complaints about loud shouts or anyone arguing or screaming, nothing like that?"

"No, nothing," he said, pulling his collar out, starting to feel like he at the very least should have heard something.

"You see the victim at any time during the night at all?" Jack asked.

The man looked shaken. "No, why should I?" he said in a defensive way.

Jack persisted. "You see anyone going into the man's room at any time during the night?"

"No! Hey, I wasn't posted right outside his door, you know. I wouldn't have had reason to even be up there unless there was a complaint, which there wasn't." His face was reddening, his speech was pressured.

"Okay, okay," Jack said soothingly. "Just trying to do my job, like you do yours."

This was met with a slight grin. "Yeah, sure, I understand," the guard said, relaxing.

"Anybody go into that room at all once the body was found?" Jack asked, glaring again.

"No way, not even me. I saw the blood, but I was only there at the doorway, so I backed off, called 911," he said, giving Jack an inquiring look.

"What about while you were calling, did anyone go into the room?"

The guard got it. "Oh, no, huh-uh. I used my radio, called downstairs, actually had them to call 911 for me, then I posted myself outside the door, waiting for you guys. That was the right thing to do, wasn't it?" he asked.

Jack nodded. "Yeah, you did good," he said, distracted, thinking.

"Just doing what I'm supposed to," the guard answered importantly.

"What time was the body actually discovered?"

Jack waited as the man pulled out a small note pad, consulted it, then said, "Eight-oh-five this morning."

Jack studied him. "What time do you go off duty?"

"Seven," the guard answered.

"But you were still here?"

"Oh, yeah. My replacement hadn't shown up, so I stayed on, waiting for him." He looked around. "That damn sombitch still hasn't showed his face. I bet he's out drunk somewhere."

Jack ignored that.

"So, you continued on duty until the body was found?"

"Hell, man, I'm still on duty," he said, sounding whiny.

"What about check-in time for this guy, around ten o'clock, the card reads. Who was on duty then?"

"Guy named Arnie Carpenter. He's on most nights."

"We'll need to talk to him," Jack said, more to himself than the guard. "See if he noticed the guy come in, anything at all about him."

"I'll get his address and number for you right now," the guard said, going toward the office.

Jack approached the desk clerk. "I'll need the name, address, and phone number of whoever signed the gentleman in upstairs," he said, pulling out his note pad.

"The manager should have that," the clerk said. "I'll go get it," and hurried away.

Jack watched the young lady's swaying bottom, going through a checklist in his mind.

Marvin came out of the office, housekeeper in tow. She was Hispanic, heavily built. Her face was red, puffy from crying. She looked green around the gills. Jack imagined it would take her a few months before the image she witnessed would begin to fade from her memory. He felt sorry for her.

"I think I got all the information I need," Marvin said, addressing him. "You got anything you want to talk to her about?"

Jack, not wanting to cause the young lady more stress than she apparently was feeling, said, "No, if I think of anything, you got her name and info?"

"Yeah, first thing," Marvin said. Then, turning to the young woman, said, his voice soft, compassionate. "We won't need you any further. Why don't you go on home, get some rest, try to forget what happened this morning?"

The housekeeper mutely nodded, then walked off, as if in a daze.

"Man, that must have been a sight for a first-timer," Marvin mused.

"Shit, it was a sight for me, and I've seen countless dead bodies," Jack said. "I'm not particularly looking forward to going back up there."

"You and me both," Marvin agreed. .

The security guard hurried up to them, importantly thrust a piece of notepaper at Jack. "Here's Arnie's address and phone," he said.

"Thanks." Jack handed it to Marvin.

27

Jack looked around the lobby. "Security cameras?" he asked, pointing to a corner of the lobby.

The guard nodded. "We only got the one, focused on the desk here, as a protective measure for our employees."

"I need the tape from nine-thirty last night through this morning at eight-oh-five."

"You got it," the guard said, then hurried away again.

Jack and Marvin saw the assistant medical examiner at the same time as she came in through the revolving doors in the lobby.

"Well, hey, lookit who we got here," Marvin said loudly.

She glanced their way, shot them both a bright smile.

They grinned back.

She came toward them, medical bag in hand, stopped in front of them, solemnly shook with them, a twinkle in her eyes.

Sara Cooper was a tall, heavyset, red-headed woman whose ruddy complexion caused people to think she was either continually blushing or running a fever, to her constant consternation. Jack and Marvin both liked working with her.

"Well, boys," she drawled, "what have you got for me this time?"

"Something real special," Marvin said, grinning widely, "something I think you're gonna enjoy."

"What are we waiting for?" she asked, heading toward the elevators.

They followed along, listening to her story about a recent case she had worked on involving a murdered woman lying over the back of a chair, one red high heel on, the other one missing. They mused about what the missing heel meant as they went toward the room.

All three stopped outside, waiting for the signal from Bogie to come on in.

He looked up, grinned, waved them in, then went back to collecting blood off the wall behind the bed.

As the ME went toward the body, Marvin and Jack advanced into the room, being careful not to tread on any evidence.

Sara read the words on the wall, then looked at the body. "I take it the Wayne is metaphorical," she said.

"I'd bet on it," Bogie agreed.

They all watched as she approached the corpse, stood staring at it.

"Well?" Jack asked, "what do you think, Sara?"

She looked up, gave him an impish smile, as she donned rubber gloves. "What do I think? I think this guy's dead, that's what I think," she said, bending over him.

CHAPTER 6

The young woman sits silently in the chair in front of the psychologist's desk, he behind it. He watches her across the narrow space, absently rubbing his chin, waiting for her to begin. He is a little put off by the fact that after the initial amenities, she has fallen quiet and has not offered him anything, which is somewhat unusual in his profession. He has found with other patients that silence seems to draw them out more. In order to fill the uncomfortable silence, they will begin to open up, share with him.

Beneath the professional facade, the man surreptitiously checks her out, appreciating the shapely legs, compact body, kissable lips, dark hair. He wonders what color her eyes are, hidden behind the sunglasses. Wonders what she feels she is protecting behind the glasses. However, the professional man won't ask her to take them off, not yet.

She sits, watching him watch her, a small smile playing across her lips.

When it is clear she will not speak first, he straightens up, leans forward slightly, clears his voice, then, glancing at the client data sheet she has provided, says, "I don't see a last name here. Is there a reason you didn't provide it?" looking back up at her.

She mimics his posture, straightening up, leaning toward him, uncrossing her legs in the process, watching him watch them. "My name is Ronnie," she says, her voice low, husky. "If you need a last name, I am not ready at this time to share with you the name of the person whose body I inhabit."

He perks up at that. She notices. He ponders a moment. "Would you like to expand on that?" he finally asks.

She smiles openly. "Doctor, please," she says, her voice condescending. He waits. She finally shrugs, then says, "I'm sure you're aware of multiple personality disorder, disassociative identity disorder, or whatever the current trendy DSM-IV diagnosis would be. I happen to be what you would call an alternate personality within the body you so obviously, shall we say, appreciate."

He frowns slightly at that, drawing a smile from her. He holds his temper in check at this, frustrated he is letting her get to him so quickly. He leans back, racking his brain for any research he has read concerning an alternate being aware enough of the disorder to seek treatment. Can't remember anything, dammit, then briefly wondering if what she has told him is not contrived.

"And you are here?" he prods.

"I am here to help her," Ronnie states flatly, "the primary persona."

"And who is she?"

"You don't need to know that now," Ronnie says, her voice harsh.

He considers this. "All right," he finally concedes. "In what way do you want to help her?"

"Wouldn't the therapeutic goal be to merge the personalities?" she asks in a mocking manner.

He counts to ten, then, ignoring this, "Are there personalities other than you and the primary that you're aware of?"

She cocks her head to one side. "Just one other, a small child who doesn't appear too often. I guess I would be considered the dominant alternate, if there is such a thing. I know I have the power to come forth at will if I exert it strongly enough."

He nods his head, encouraging her to continue.

"Such as at times like this," she says, flipping her hand, indicating his office.

"What happens to her, the host," he asks, "at times like this?"

Ronnie shrugs. "She's very unhappy over all this," she finally answers. "When I come forth, she just goes to sleep, I guess, goes away, whatever, and when I allow her to take control back, it leaves her very confused. She doesn't know where the time has gone, where she has been, what she has done, et cetera. She's thinking about getting help herself, but I'd rather be the one to choose the therapist. I don't trust her to do the right thing."

He is intrigued now, his interest overriding his anger at her. "That's why you're here?"

"Yes, of course. But one caveat, Doctor. I would like for her to merge with me. I would like to be the primary, not the alternate. You see, she's a weakling, soft, vulnerable. She can't take care of herself. She can't keep herself safe. That's why I exist. That's what I do, protect her, and I must tell you, it's getting awfully boring."

31

He leans back, rubbing his chin again. "And is that when you first split, protecting her?"

She smiles openly. "Of course. Very textbook, would you not agree?"

He decides not to answer that. "Can you tell me the circumstances?"

"Let's just say she had a terrible childhood," she says after a moment's pause.

"Can you be more specific than that?" he asks, thinking, *Didn't we all.*

She shrugs. "Typical story, I suppose. Of primary importance is the abusive father. Oh, he did terrible things to her."

"Such as?"

"Physical abuse, sexual abuse, emotional abuse, you name it, he did it."

He nods his head, indicating go on.

She settles back, seems happy to tell the story. "He was a jurist, well-known in the community, well-respected, well-liked." She laughs harshly. "If only anyone knew what he did to her, what she had to endure at his hands. Suffice it to say he would physically punish her severely for some contrived thing, and then afterwards, as she lay there weeping and hurting from the punishment, he would put his hands on her, touching her, rubbing her. As she matured, the touching and rubbing became penetration, first with the fingers, then with his penis. After the penetration came forcing her to touch him, to put her mouth on him." She stops, shaking her head. "She just couldn't take it, couldn't cope, poor thing. She was too weak. So, I stepped forward, took it for her, but I didn't cry. Never. And eventually, when the time was right, I took care of him and the mother, too. Made sure he wouldn't ever touch her again and the mother wouldn't ever allow it again." She pauses, thinking. "I think that's when I really became strong," she says.

She stops, watching him, then rises. "Well, my time is up, Doctor. Will you accept me as a patient?" smiling engagingly this time.

He stands. "Of course," realizing he wants her to stay, surprised at this, usually more than ready for his patients to leave when the time comes.

She offers her hand, they shake.

"We now have a doctor-patient relationship?" she asks.

"Yes," he says, wondering why she would ask this.

"So, anything I tell you will be strictly confidential, between us?" she presses.

"Yes, of course. I won't reveal what you tell me unless you specifically request that I do."

She nods her head thoughtfully, then smiles brightly again. "Good," she says, then leaning close to him, dropping her voice to barely above a whisper. "Because I have a lot to tell you, Doctor," sliding the glasses down her nose long enough for him to catch a glimmer of green ice, then back up, turning her back on him, out the door before he has a chance to react.

CHAPTER 7

A meeting of protocol was scheduled the afternoon after the corpse was found to go over what had been found at the hotel and determine whether or not to release the crime scene. Jack, Marvin, Bogie, and his two assistants made small talk while they waited for Robin and their homicide chief to make their appearance.

Robin came into the room, followed by Sgt. McKinley, a short, lean guy with blond-gray hair cut in a burr and twinkly blue eyes, known more for his personality than his methods.

Robin sat down from Jack, a gleam in her eyes. "Found out who the victim was," she said smugly.

Everybody straightened up.

"Lawyer goes by the name of Arthur Walters," she said, answering their unspoken questions. Then, further answering, "His wife called missing persons late this morning. Said he didn't come home last night and his office called her this morning because he didn't show up for a nine a.m. appointment."

"You confirmed?" their sergeant asked.

"Yep. Met her at the morgue, did the TV monitor thing, and she said it was her hubby," Robin said, then, "If it counts for anything, she didn't look too saddened by his death," glancing at Jack.

Everybody thought this over for a moment.

"Maybe she did him," Marvin said.

"Nah, she looked like she couldn't stand to get her little pinky dirty," Robin said, "much less all that blood."

"Those bitches are the worst ones," Marvin said.

Everyone laughed.

"An attorney-at-law," their sergeant said, a grin playing around his mouth. "Now, surely it won't be hard finding whoever got it in their little old heart to do us all a favor and take a lawyer out of our world."

They all grinned.

"Yeah, but, see, the problem is, there'll probably be a line a mile long," Marvin said.

"Anybody know what kind of lawyer?" Bogie asked.

They looked at him.

"You know, tax lawyer, patent lawyer, defense lawyer, plaintiff's lawyer?"

"I'll be right back," Robin said, leaving the room.

"Criminal lawyer, we're gonna be doing a whole hell of a lot of digging," Marvin said.

"Didn't look like a criminal lawyer to me," Jack said. "Didn't mix his polka dots with plaid."

Everyone laughed again.

Robin came back in. "Corporate lawyer," she said, taking her seat. "One of the biggest firms in Knoxville. And the dude was a senior partner." She raised her eyebrows.

"All righty, then," their sergeant said, leaning toward them. "Makes our job a little bit easier, we hope." He looked toward Bogie. "Okay, Boge, your nose tell you anything this morning?" They all grinned. Unlike everyone else at a homicide crime scene, Bogie never placed a handkerchief over or put salve under his nose to hide the smell. He had an olfactory sense like a bloodhound and was notoriously known for being able to pilfer out smells other than death.

"Scent in the bathroom," Bogie said. "Kind of cinnamony, I think."

Everybody gave him a respectful look.

"Girlfriend's maybe," Jack said.

"Or hooker's," Marvin interjected.

"Probably the wife's. You-all know what the stats are on that," Sgt. McKinley said.

"Could be a man's," Robin said.

"Smelled more feminine to me, more sweet than spice," Bogie added.

"What else you got, Bogie?" the sergeant asked.

"Nada as of yet. Of course, we'll go through everything we collected at the scene, but so far, no prints, no nothing that's discernible. Nothing in the garbage cans. Glasses only had one set of prints on them, and I'll bet next month's paycheck they're the victim's."

The sergeant looked at Jack. "Anybody see or hear anything?" he asked, knowing the answer beforehand.

Jack shook his head.

"Anybody got any idea who Wayne is?" he asked.

Everyone was silent.

He turned to Robin. "Happen to know if Wayne was this guy Walters' middle name?"

She smiled. "Nope," she answered. "Not his middle name, nor nickname. His wife says no one's ever referred to Arthur," saying this arrogantly, "as Wayne," saying this with contempt. "That's the way she said it, too," she added, nodding her head.

"We ready to release the crime scene?" the sergeant asked, looking toward Bogie.

Bogie shook his head. "I want to go back over there in the morning, look around again."

"He means sniff around," Marvin said.

Bogie shrugged. "Never can tell, we might have overlooked something, although I doubt it."

"When's the autopsy?" McKinley asked.

"Tomorrow afternoon," Bogie replied.

"Of course Bogie will be there. We all know how he loves to watch dead bodies get hacked to pieces. Jack, you or Marvin want to sit in on that?"

They both shook their heads. "I'll wait on Bogie's report," Jack said.

"Okay, we got us one dead lawyer sans left testicle," McKinley said. Everybody laughed. "You guys know what to do, so I suggest you get on it," he groused, getting up.

Jack, Marvin, and Robin stayed behind. Jack turned to Robin. "I hate to do this to you, but do you mind going back and interviewing Ms. Walters in detail? See what you can find out?"

Robin frowned at him. "You would give me the shittiest job."

They glared at each other. Finally, Jack sighed, then said, his voice acerbic. "It just makes more sense to me, Robin. She's familiar with you and women tend to open up more to other women, or at least that seems to be the case to me. You females can handle these situations in a more sensitive fashion than us guys seem to be able to do. But hey, you got a problem with it, I'll take care of it."

Marvin watched all this with interest.

Robin glared some more, then turned around and left. Jack turned to Marvin. "Okay, why don't you – "

"You did it with that girl, didn't you?" Marvin accused, his eyes dancing.

"I don't know what you mean by 'did it,'" Jack growled.

"Yeah you do," Marvin said, grinning, making an obscene gesture with his hand.

Now Jack glared at Marvin. "Who I sleep with is none of your business," he said.

"Only reason I can think of she's so pissed at you. What'd you do, white man, spit your seed too early? Roll over and go to sleep? Get up in the middle of the night and sneak out?"

Jack visibly bristled.

"Well, you gonna tell me or not?" Marvin asked, his voice affable.

Ignoring this, Jack said, teeth gritted, "Why don't you go over to Walters' office, interview the office personnel there, see if anyone can tell you right off the bat who had it in for this guy? See who had contact with him during his last hours and interview them. You know the procedure."

"Yeah, and sell me some swamp land in Florida while they're at it," Marvin said, heading toward the door.

Jack went back to his desk to start the mounds of paperwork he knew this was going to involve.

CHAPTER 8

The next afternoon, Jack was sitting at his desk, going through his file, which was already collecting papers, wondering when the hell Bogie was going to give him his report on the murder at the Hyatt, when Marvin plopped down in the chair beside his desk. Jack glanced at him, grinning at the grin Marvin was giving him.

"I am in love, man," Marvin said, closing his eyes, shaking his head.

"Hope you're talking about your wife," Jack said, going back to his work.

Marvin looked surprised. "Oh, her. Well, yeah, I do love her. I do. But I wasn't talking about her." He leaned conspiratorially toward Jack. "I went down to the courthouse, interviewed that court reporter that was seen with Mr. Attorney with Missing Left Nut before he got offed, and man, talk about a looker. Ummm-ummm, good."

"Yeah?" Jack asked, egging him on.

"Man, oh, man, what I wouldn't give for a piece of that," Marvin said. "Shit, man, she's just a little, bitty thing. Small, you know, tiny. Made me feel like one big mother fucker just standing next to her. Like I coulda just eat her up if I had wanted to."

Jack grinned, settling back in his chair.

"And a white girl, too." Marvin said, then seeing Jack's look, nodded his head. "Yeah, I know, I know. I don't usually go for the white chicks, all that pale skin and all, but this one's different. Cute as hell, and yeah, I know, I like the big tits, too, and she ain't got those, but man, oh, man, what she's got. Umm-umm." He licked his lips.

"Let me write this down," Jack said, pulling over a pencil and his notebook.

"I ain't shittin you, man," Marvin said. "She's got these cat eyes. Big, green, with long black lashes all around 'em. Got this little cat face, you know, pink lips turned up like maybe she's smiling at you when she ain't. Sleek, little body. Oh, and red hair. Copper-colored hair, about the prettiest hair I reckon I've ever seen."

"Yeah?" Jack said.

"Name's Gillian. Ain't that a pretty name?" Marvin asked.

"You happen to remember anything this cat-woman might have told you that would help us find our killer?" Jack asked, getting tired of Marvin's nonsense.

Marvin shook his head. "Nothing, man. She didn't have anything to give us."

"You were probably too busy trying to work your way into her pants to find that out."

"Hey, man, I was a gentleman, I swear. Didn't make any untoward comments toward her, acted like the professional I am."

Jack burst out laughing.

"Seriously, man. Oh, but she is a sweet little thing. Looks and acts as innocent as a virgin. Hell, man, she just might be one. I could help her with that, you know."

"Like your wife would let you," Jack said. It was well known within the department that for all Marvin's posturing, his wife was the one who called the shots in his life.

Marvin's face fell. "Oh, yeah. Well, a guy can always dream, can't he?" he asked Jack, grinning again. "Ain't nothing wrong with fantasizing about another woman."

"Sure, there's not," Jack replied affably. "In fact, your wife probably fantasizes about other guys, so, you know, all's fair."

Marvin's eyes narrowed. "Say what?" he said, his voice going higher. "Huh-uh. No way. My wife has got all the man she needs right here. She don't need to go fantasizing about some other dude when she's got me."

"I wonder if she fantasizes about us white guys," Jack said, a grin playing around his mouth.

"Man, you're crazy. That woman don't fantasize 'bout nobody but her man, as in me, Mar-Vin, you dig?"

Jack gave him a challenging stare. "You so sure about that?"

Marvin's face fell. "Well, I tell you what, I'm gonna find out. I'm gonna call that bitch right now and ask her, and she better not be fantasizing about any other dude, especially some shithead white-ass dude, or she gonna have the wrath of Marvin come down on her head, believe me."

He stomped off toward his desk.

Jack's phone rang. He picked it up, irritated, wanting to

eavesdrop on the conversation between Marvin and his mate.

"Daniels," he said crisply.

"Jackson," Bogie's dry voice came over the line.

"Hey, Bogie," Jack said, pulling his pad closer. "What you got for me?"

Bogie sighed. *Shit*, thought Jack.

"I'll start with the autopsy," Bogie said. "Preliminarily, it's pretty safe to say the guy died from a puncture wound to the heart."

"That was pretty obvious," Jack said, writing.

"Yeah, but as we both know, guy, a lot of times the most obvious turns out not to be the obvious."

"True," Jack said.

"As for forensic evidence, we got all kinds going nowhere," Bogie continued. "This was a hotel room, you know. Vacuumed up all kinds of fibers and hairs from probably countless people. Same with fingerprints. The alternate light source wasn't much good. No hairs or fibers other than the victim's or the sheets from the bed. Even the pubic comb didn't produce anything. However, there are a few interesting things you might want to consider."

"As in?" Jack asked, rubbing his neck.

"As in the writing on the wall. Of course, there was so much blood trailing down, it'll make it near impossible to ever match that up with anything."

"Of course," Jack agreed.

"But as an aside, the instrument used to write 'Wayne's Dead' with was none other than . . ."

"The guy's left nut," Jack answered.

"Which was severed, we're pretty sure, with a scalpel," Bogie added.

"Ouch," Jack said, then, "Those are pretty easy to get hold of, huh?"

"All these medical supply places around, just about anybody can get one," Bogie answered, both thinking the same thing: no way they could trace a scalpel.

"Wonder who Wayne is, anyway," Bogie said.

"Sure ain't the guy who was laying on that bed," Jack answered.

"At least he went happy," Bogie offered.

"What makes you say that?"

"He ejaculated prior to death, so at least it wasn't all for naught."

"You're one sick puppy," Jack said.

Bogie offered a soft chuckle at this. "Did you notice anything about the toilet seat?"

Jack thought. "No, not really."

"It was down."

Jack sat there. "So?" he finally asked.

"Well, that usually indicates the last one to use the toilet was a woman."

"Or a man trained by a woman to put it down," Jack said.

"True."

"Or maybe no one used the toilet at all. No, wait, the sanitary strip wasn't on the toilet, was it, it was in the trash can."

"Right."

"Hey, Bogie, you trying to tell me you think our killer's a woman?" Jack said into the phone, his voice low.

"Maybe," Bogie replied.

"I don't think so. All that blood, plus the mutilation factor. Statistically speaking, women are cleaner killers than men, right?"

"That's what the stats say, but I got to tell you, big guy, that ain't exactly been my experience," Bogie replied drily.

Jack thought. "Still, all that blood, all that violence. Hey, that reminds me. Was he dead before the mutilation or after?"

He heard Bogie rummaging through papers. "I would say that with all that blood, he was probably still alive, Jack, but probably just barely," he said into the phone.

Jack shook his head. "Feels like a man to me, Boge," he said.

They thought a minute. "Maybe this guy had a rendezvous with a woman and her husband found out about it," Bogie said.

"Yeah, could be. Or maybe he was gay and had a male lover there."

"No indication of anal intercourse," Bogie said.

"With him," Jack replied. "We don't know about the partner."

"You gonna follow up on that?" Bogie asked.

"Bogie, I am gonna follow everything imaginable," Jack answered, then, "What else?"

"Little makeup smear on the victim's face. Also some lipstick smear on the body, the abdomen and the mouth."

41

"Hmmm," Jack said.

"But don't get your hopes up. No way you can trace that back to any one person. Hell, could have even come from the guy's wife for all we know. Makeup and lipstick are made up in lots, by the thousands. Impossible to try to track that down."

"Damn," Jack said.

"My feelings exactly," Bogie replied. Then, "Did get a partial palm print off the body. I guess the perp left it when he or she forced whatever instrument of maim was used to kill the guy with."

"You figured out what could have caused the puncture wound into the heart?"

"No, but I'm working on it," Bogie answered.

"Any match on the palm print?" Jack asked.

"What do you think?" Bogie said, his voice sarcastic.

Jack sighed, sitting back. "No fingerprints at all on the body, anywhere?"

"Nothing definite, but of course, as we both know, the perp could have been taking some sort of illegal drugs or antihistamines that would dry up the oils in the skin, makes getting a good print almost impossible."

Jack sat there, replaying the crime scene in his mind, wondering if he had missed something.

"There is one puzzling aspect here," Bogie offered.

"Yeah?"

"As pertains to the condom which we found on the body, even though there was seminal fluid contained inside, there was no evidence of any sort of body fluid on the outside."

"Huh," Jack said.

"My thoughts exactly."

"You mean, no vaginal secretions, nothing?"

"Nada."

"You're not telling me the guy masturbated with a condom on, are you?"

Bogie was silent a moment, then said, "I don't know what to make of it, to tell you the truth. You would expect something left behind, either from a woman's body or a man's, but there is nothing on it, the damn thing's clean as a whistle."

"Jeez," Jack said, "that sure is something to puzzle out."

Bogie laughed into the phone. "One of your favorite things to do, guy. I'll have the report sent to you by the a.m."

"Thanks, Boge," Jack said, putting the phone down, thinking.

CHAPTER 9

Jackson and Marvin were in a nondescript police sedan, heading toward the home of Attorney Walters' widow.

"I thought Robin already did this," Marvin said in a complaining tone, watching the Tennessee River whiz by.

"Yeah, but there's something she didn't go into that she should have," Jack said.

"As in?"

"Was this guy straight or gay."

"How you gonna approach that, man?" Marvin asked, his attention on Jack now.

"Approach what?"

"Query this woman about was her old man a faggot or not," Marvin answered, grinning.

Jack gave him a look. "Oh. Gee, I hadn't thought about that, Marvin. How would you go about that, you being the professional inquisitor you are?"

"Oh, the man's being sarcastic. Okay. All right. You go on and take out whatever ill feelings you're having this beautiful day about whatever or whoever on your old buddy Marvin here, okay? Just go right on ahead, and I'll take it 'cause you know what? I, unlike most of the other people on this planet, can take it."

"Actually, I hadn't thought about it," Jack said. "I guess I'll just play it by ear. That is, unless you want to broach the subject yourself."

"Nuh-uh, no way. You know I don't go anywhere near that subject," Marvin said. "Shit, people get testy you go asking them about their sex life."

"Don't I know it," Jack said.

They pulled into the drive of a huge, three-story tudor in an old, monied part of Knoxville near the river.

"Damn, take a gander at this abode," Marvin said, his voice low, looking the place over.

"The guy had money," Jack said.

"Man, oh, man, can you imagine living in a house like this?"

44

Marvin asked. "Damn, dude, you'd have to ride a golf cart just to get from one end to the other, what you say?"

"I say, no thanks," Jack said, opening his door. "I got better things to spend my money on than living space not being occupied."

"Ain't that the truth," Marvin said, getting out.

They walked side by side to the entrance. "This gonna be one of those good cop, bad cop things?" Marvin asked.

Jack grinned. "Marvin, why you always wanting to play the bad cop?" he teased. "Man, you know that doesn't work. How many times I got to tell you that?"

"Just thought I'd see," Marvin said, ringing the bell.

A young Hispanic maid in a severe black outfit with a white, lacy apron answered their knock and, upon properly asking for and then seeing their IDs, escorted them into what she called the "library," ignoring Marvin's blatant attempts to engage her in some serious flirting.

"So this is what they call a library, huh?" Marvin asked, walking about, surveying the book-lined shelves, which occupied all the wall space.

Jack ignored him, standing in the middle of the room waiting.

After several minutes, a middle-aged woman dressed in a blue, raw-silk running suit breezed into the room in a busy manner. Her hair was gray, her build was stocky, her demeanor harried.

"Gentlemen," she said, heading toward a chair in front of the fireplace, indicating with a wave of the hand for them to sit on the couch across from her, then pointedly looking at her watch. Jack got the message.

After assuming their positions, Jackson leaned toward her. "Before we begin, we'd like to say that we're sorry for your loss, ma'am," he said, his voice low.

She nodded her head without replying. Jack studied her a moment. She did not appear to be a grieving widow to him. Hostile, maybe. Not grief-stricken though.

"We just have a few questions we need to ask concerning your late husband," he said.

"I have already been interviewed by your department," she said nastily. "I can't imagine what else you would want me to tell you."

Okay, Jack thought, *go for the jugular*. "Ma'am, would you like

45

to call your attorney?" he asked, glaring at her, his eyes hard.

She responded as he had hoped she would, now looking not as hostile, not as confident, wondering, he was sure, if they had pegged her as a suspect, her eyes darting to Marvin, then back to Jack.

She straightened in her chair, then said, trying for a haughty tone but failing mightily, "Do I need to call my lawyer, gentlemen?"

"That's your choice, Ms. Walters," Jack said, leaning back in his chair, studying her.

She glared at him, then finally said, "I have nothing to hide from you, ask whatever it is you need to," waving her hand in dismissal.

Jack nodded, waiting a moment, letting her squirm first. "Simply put, Ms. Walters, was your husband having an affair at the time of his death?" Jack finally asked, staring at her, waiting for her reaction.

Her face changed. Now she looked, what, chagrined, maybe. *Huh,* Jack thought, *maybe her husband wasn't the only one fooling around.*

"Not that I know of," she replied curtly.

"He didn't tell you he was going to the Hyatt that night?" Marvin asked, watching her quizzically.

"No, of course not," she replied in an indignant way.

"Did he say where he was going or would be?" Jackson asked.

She looked away, then back, giving him a hateful look. "My husband and I weren't the sort of couple who kept track of each other's movements, moment by moment."

Jack raised his eyebrows, sat back.

"I mean," she said, somewhat hurriedly, "I knew he would be home that evening, sometime. We had an agreement, an arrangement. We were married, but we didn't actually . . . we weren't like the average married couple, I suppose you could say."

Jack and Marvin sat there, waiting.

She seemed to grow uncomfortable, her face reddening. She grimaced, then said, "Art and I were no longer intimate with each other and agreed quite some time ago to remain married but to be, well, free to consider other possibilities outside of the marital relationship with the caveat that we each be discrete, of course, concerning other possible partners."

"In other words, you didn't question each other concerning other intimate relationships," Jackson said.

"Yes, quite right. Art went his way, I went mine. My word, we've been . . . we'd been married twenty-five years. What was the point, you see. He had his life, I had mine."

Jackson didn't see. He shot Marvin a look.

"So, were you aware your husband was having an affair or weren't you?" Marvin asked.

"Well, Art had his little flings. He's always had his little flings. They were nothing to me. I never thought anything of them. Well, maybe relief. It kept him away from me." She stopped, looking guilty. "We weren't compatible, I suppose," she said, her voice dropping.

Jack said, "Did you know if your husband was seeing anyone in particular at the time of his death?"

She thought a moment, then shook her head. "As I said, I didn't think anything of his little affairs. I couldn't have cared less, to tell you the truth. Of course, I'd say he probably was seeing someone. I just couldn't tell you who. I never asked." She shrugged, giving them a slight smile.

Jesus, Jackson thought.

He leaned toward her. "Ms. Walters, please understand I'm trying to investigate who may have actually murdered your husband, so I would appreciate anything you could tell me."

"But I can't offer you anything," she protested, her voice strained. "I didn't know, I didn't care. It's as simple as that. It's bad enough the whole world will know how he died and where. That bastard should have known better. I thought he was more discrete than that! He had promised me that much! I thought he had more sense than to end up in a hotel room, murdered, sprawled naked on a bed for the whole damn world to see!" Her face had turned red, her speech was pressured. She stopped abruptly, visibly fighting to control herself.

Jack and Marvin glanced at each other.

"Ma'am," Jack said, "please understand I'm only doing my job when I ask you this, but was your husband gay or bisexual? Were you aware of any – "

"Get out of my house!" she yelled, standing up. "How dare you come here and insult me as to Arthur's sexual proclivities. I'll sue you and the whole damn police department if you even hint to the press that you suspect Arthur – "

"Hey, now," Marvin said, his voice soothing. "We're not insinuating anything here, Ms. Walters. We're just trying to find out who killed him, you know, a man or a woman, and then go from there. That's all. I promise."

She sat down abruptly, her face bright red, took a few deep breaths, calming herself, then looked Jackson in the face, hatred evident in her eyes. "Arthur Walters was a heterosexual, officer, pure and simple. Why, he'd probably rather fuck a pig than another man, if you want the truth." With that, she got up and walked toward the door.

"Ms. Walters," Jack said, his voice mild.

She stopped but didn't turn around, keeping her back to them, waiting.

"We can do this here or we can go down to the police station and do it there, it's your choice," he continued, watching her stiffen at that. "My partner and I are here to ask you questions concerning your husband, and I apologize if they make you uncomfortable, but they need to be asked. We're investigating his death and the least you can do out of respect for him is sit here and talk to us."

She seemed to take her time turning around and coming toward them. Jack noticed her face was flushed, her eyes bright.

She sat down, giving Jack a hostile look, then turning her attention to Marvin.

Jack sat back, indicating for Marvin to take it.

"Ms. Walters, you are telling us that to your knowledge, your husband did not engage in any homosexual experiences?" Marvin asked again.

She glared, then said, "My husband was in no way a homosexual, officer," between gritted teeth.

Marvin nodded, then said, "All right, ma'am, thank you," his voice soothing.

Jack thought a moment, then asked, "Did he like to be called by any name other than his actual name, Arthur Benning Walters?"

She shook her head. "I've already been asked that, but no, everyone called him Art."

"Ma'am, I'll put this as delicately as I can, but what about as regards his private organ, some men have names for them. Did Mr. Walters have – "

"No, of course not," she said, her face reddening, then, "at least that I'm aware of."

Jack leaned toward her. "What about unusual sexual preferences, anything along that line?" he asked her.

She bristled visibly.

"Ma'am," Marvin encouraged.

She breathed deeply for several seconds, then said, "My husband and I had not engaged in a marital relationship, as you referred to it, for many years. I can only speak as to how he was when we were intimate."

"That's fine," Marvin said, his voice soothing.

"Arthur was, I suppose, a conservative lover," she finally said, sitting rigidly in her chair. "Not one to experiment or do anything out of the ordinary, I would say; not very passionate or considerate, if the truth be known." She seemed to think a moment. "That's one of the reasons . . ." then stopped, seeming embarrassed.

"So your husband wasn't interested in sadism/masochism, bondage and discipline, anything like that?" Jack asked.

She ignored him, continuing to look at Marvin. "My husband was not that sort of person," she said, her voice harsh.

Jackson thought a moment, then said, "Ms. Walters, if you hadn't been intimate with your husband for howsoever long it was, how can you say with any degree of certainty what exactly he was interested in, whether it was sex with another man or in a different way?"

She shot up out of her chair, glaring at him. "I've said all I need to say on the subject," turned on her heel, and left.

They sat there in silence a moment, then Marvin said, "Man, I tell you what, I would not call that woman a grieving widow, what say?"

"More like a hostile one," Jack said. "I guess old Art has put the family name to shame." He shrugged, then rising said, "Well, Marvin, you got your wish."

"You mind telling me what the hell you're talking about?" Marvin asked, walking beside him toward the door.

Jackson stopped, turned to him. "Was it my imagination or weren't you doing the good cop routine a few minutes ago?"

"Shit, man, you know I'm the bad cop," Marvin said, heading toward the door. "How many times I got to tell you I'm one mean mother, Jackson?"

49

Jack trailed behind, grinning.

They got back in the car. Jack sat there, brooding.

"Well, you gonna start the car or we gonna sit here all day?" Marvin asked grouchily.

"You think she could have done it?" Jack asked.

"Nah, man, her alibi checked out," Marvin said. "Was spending the night with her daughter, who's pregnant and whose hubby was out of town. Daughter says they slept in the same bed together, seeing as they only got the one bedroom, and mommy dearest was there all night. Besides, I'd say she was living the good life with old Art the Fart. Didn't have to worry about having sex with him, had his permission to do her own thing while he supported her ass. I'd say life for her was pretty good before Artie boy got hooked up with the wrong lover."

Jack nodded. "But if she's the beneficiary of all this," he said, waving his hand toward the house, "life's gonna be even better, wouldn't you say?"

Marvin nodded. "Yeah, but, like I told you, her alibi's tight, man, it wasn't her. Besides, like you said, Art has shamed the family name. That woman seemed more concerned with how he died than the fact that the dude's dead. I get the feeling if he had been killed cleanly, you know, a nice shot to the head or a heart attack, maybe, she'd be happy as a pig rolling around in a pile of manure."

"You never did tell me what the cat-woman said," Jack segued, starting the car up.

"Oh, yeah. Said she took depositions for him late that afternoon and afterwards he walked her out of the building, asked her to go for a drink with him, but she had other plans, so they split there on the street. She never saw him again."

Jack nodded his head, then glanced at his partner. "You think she may have been the affair?"

Marvin grinned. "Shit, no, man. That girl's got class. Plus cute as hell. What would she want with an over-the-hill, pot-bellied attorney at law? Man, I bet she's got dudes coming onto her all day long."

Jack nodded his head, pulling out of the drive. He snuck a glance at Marvin. "So, what'd you find out from your wife, buddy?" he asked, a smile playing around his lips.

Marvin looked at him. "Oh, you be talking about the fantasizing thing, right? Man, I told you, that woman don't do no fantasizing about nothing or nobody but her man, period. And just to make sure, when I get home tonight, I'm gonna give her a good dose of the Marvin Mo-chine, gonna turn her inside out, give her something to fantasize about for the next hundred years."

"Yeah, right," Jack said, grinning.

CHAPTER 10

"Jackson Daniels," he said into the phone, after listening to the desk sergeant tell him there was a young lady wanting to see someone about the attorney who got killed.

"Send her up," Jack said, putting the phone down, leaning back in his chair, warily wondering if this was another one of the crazies who seemed to come out of the woodwork with each murder, offering all kinds of useless, needless, delusional information.

Straightened up in his chair when a woman with hair the color of copper walked into the room, looking around uncomfortably. He studied her as two officers raced each other to get to her, wondering if this was the court reporter Marvin had told him about. The one with the cat eyes.

He watched as both officers hovered around her, offering assistance. Jack noticed her cool detachment, thinking she must be used to getting all kinds of unwanted attention, looking like that, as her eyes met his and she broke away from the men and approached him.

He stood as she came near. "Can I help you?" he asked, looking into her eyes, thinking, *Yep, this has got to be her, the one got Marvin so riled up.*

"I came to talk to a detective named Marvin Witherspoon," she said, her voice soft, "but they told me he wasn't here and you could help me."

He held out his hand. "I'm Jackson Daniels, I'll be glad to help in any way I can."

She gave him a smile of relief as they shook. He felt huge standing beside her, taking note of how small and compact her body was, how mightily fine it was put together.

"Please, have a seat," he said, pulling a chair out for her.

"Thank you," she replied primly, sitting down.

He watched with interest as her skirt rode up her thigh, then glanced away when she tugged it down.

Jack sat down at his desk, looked up and around the room, watching all the men watch her, narrowed his eyes at them, indicating get to work, then smiled inwardly when they scurried to look busy.

They looked at each other. *Not only a cat's eyes, but a cat's face,* he thought, noting the triangular shape, wide, green eyes, small nose, pink lips, appreciating Marvin's taste for once.

He smiled, trying to put her at ease. She smiled uneasily back. "So, what can I do for you?" he asked.

"Well, the detective who interviewed me about the – oh, I'm sorry, I didn't introduce myself. I'm Gillian McKenzie."

He liked that name, wondered if she was Irish. *Of course she is,* he told himself, *with that hair and those eyes.*

"Anyway, he told me," she went on, "that if I thought of anything that might be, well, relative to your investigation into the – the death of Mr. Walters, however benign, to be sure and let y'all know."

Southern girl, he thought, nodding his head, encouraging her to go on.

"It's nothing, really, but . . ."

"What may be nothing to you, Ms. McKenzie – "

"Please, call me Gillian or Gill," she said quickly.

"Pretty name," he said.

"So's Jackson," she replied. Then, "Oh, no offense at the word pretty, but I like that. It's different."

"Thanks," he said, smiling, liking the fact she liked his name.

They stared at each other for a moment. She broke it, looking away. "Anyway, I wasn't really sure what sort of information y'all were looking for, but it occurred to me just knowing something about his character might help you find the killer."

Jack nodded his head.

She gave him a pained look, then continued. "See, Mr. Walters was – well, I guess you'd call him a lady's man." She grimaced. "I myself would consider him a lecherous old fart."

Jack grinned at that.

She looked embarrassed. "I shouldn't speak ill of the dead, I guess, but he was always coming on to me. Well, not only me, but others as well, always trying to flirt – well, actually more than that." She shrugged. "He propositioned me more than once, and I was thinking about that last night and thought maybe he happened to proposition the wrong person, you know, that night." She gave Jack a questioning look.

He nodded his head, thinking how absolutely gorgeous this little lass was.

"The really disturbing thing," she continued, "was that he seemed to feel he could be at liberty to do things that I wouldn't consider proper."

Jack perked up at this, pulling his notebook closer, grabbing up a pen. "Such as?"

She seemed to blush slightly. "Well, he would whisper things, sometimes, personal things, tell me he would like to do certain sexual things with me when we were alone. At times, it seemed as if he felt I would go along with what he wanted, I would be open to his suggestions, as if he seemed to think we were involved in some way, which we weren't. He made me very uncomfortable, so I made sure I was never alone with him. I even screened my calls so I wouldn't have to talk to him."

"He called you?" Jack asked.

"Yes. At home. When it happened the first time, you know, when he started saying things to me, I cut him off, told him someone was at the door, and from then on, used my service for all my calls."

Jack was busy writing. "Did he make sexual advances toward you?"

She shook her head no. "Not physically. Like I said, I was never alone with him, but when we would be in the same room or on an elevator, he would do that, lean over, start whispering in my ear." She shuddered slightly. "It was creepy. Almost like he thought we were lovers."

"How would you respond when he did this?" Jack asked, curious.

"I just ignored him for the most part, acted like I didn't hear him, but it didn't stop him from continuing to do that."

"Yet you took depositions for him the day he was killed," Jack said.

She shook her head yes. "A friend of mine who's a court reporter and who had booked that depo got sick and called me that morning, asking me to fill in for her. I did it as a favor, not knowing he would be there. I could have kicked myself for not asking who the attorneys were before I agreed to take the deposition."

They locked eyes. Jack pretended to be thinking while studying her. She just stared back impassively. Her hair had been pulled into a braid that fell partially down her back. Wisps of copper curled around her face, seeming to frame it.

"You have really beautiful eyes," she said, surprising him. He felt his eyebrows go up, wondering if she was flirting with him.

"I'm sorry, I probably shouldn't have said that," she said, appearing flustered.

"No, no, it's okay," he said, giving her a small grin. "In fact, I was just thinking the same thing about you," he admitted.

They smiled at each other.

"Anyway," she said, once more breaking contact, "I thought that may be something the police should know. I mean, like I said, maybe he propositioned the wrong person. If he was doing things like that to me, I'm sure he was to other women, as well. God knows, I felt almost relief when I found out he was dead."

She seemed to realize what she had relayed, giving Jack a startled look.

"Can't blame you for feeling like that," he said.

Jack thought a moment, then asked, "Did Mr. Walters ever do or say anything or did you ever hear anything that would give you any indication he may have been involved with anyone else specifically?"

She thought, then said, "No, never. He always seemed so focused on me when we were together, to tell you the truth. At least, that's all he seemed to want to talk about."

"Did you ever notice or hear that Mr. Walters may have been harassing anyone else in the same manner he was you?" Jack asked.

"I sure hope not. Like I said, it was very uncomfortable. I almost got to the point where I was afraid to go anywhere, for fear I'd have to deal with him."

"Did he ever do or say anything that would indicate to you he may have been inclined toward homosexuality, or possibly that he was bisexual?" Jack asked.

Gillian smiled as if she thought Jack was crazy. "Mr. Walters? Shoot, I never would have thought that about him. He was the type of guy that was always watching women, you know? He'd be talking to another person but his eyes would be on a woman somewhere, watching her. He was lecherous and creepy and, to tell you the truth, the most repulsive man I've ever known; but no, I never saw any indication he was interested in anything other than the female gender."

"Well, I'm glad you told me what you did," Jack said. "You never know, this could be very important."

He sat there, rubbing his chin, appearing to be thinking while appreciating her. He finally leaned toward her, said, "Is there anything else you can tell me?"

Gillian shook her head no, looking almost disappointed. So was he.

"So, do you think you might like to go for coffee?" Jack asked.

She gave him an impish grin, then said, "I'm really glad Mr. Witherspoon wasn't here." They smiled at each other.

They stood outside her apartment door. By the time they had left the police department, it was late, so he had followed her to her apartment, waited while she parked her car, then they had gone to a restaurant for a meal instead of just coffee.

During the meal, she had kept the topic on him, managing to turn the subject away from her each time he tried. He was intrigued by her guardedness, thinking he hadn't actually found out anything about her life, while she knew his front to back.

She smiled slightly, then said, her voice low, "I don't normally ask men in after just meeting them, but would you like to?"

God, yes, he thought as he nodded his head.

She smiled as if happy at this, then inserted her key and he followed her in.

"Would you like something to drink?" she asked, flipping a switch by the door, illuminating the room with a white pottery lamp near the window.

"Sure, whatever you're drinking," Jack said, stepping into the room, looking around.

At first glance, everything seemed white, cottony, pillowy. As his eyes adjusted to the light, he picked up soft muted colors in the throw pillows on the couch, afghan draped over an overstuffed chair, silk flowers on the white coffee table.

However, the white overshadowed all. Jack almost felt like he was adrift in a cloud, standing on white carpet, buffeted by white walls, white furniture.

Gillian watched him as he studied the room, a small smile playing at her lips.

"How does it make you feel?" she asked, her voice teasing.

"Like I'm in the air," he said.

She smiled as if pleased. "Why don't you make yourself comfortable?" she asked, then headed toward what he took to be the kitchen.

Jack plopped down on the white sofa, sinking inches into the cushions, glanced around again, thinking he liked all this white. It looked so, well, clean was the word, he guessed.

He listened as she moved around the kitchen, thinking he had never felt so attracted to a woman before as he was to her. At least, not right off. Not before the sex.

God, she was gorgeous with those dark-green eyes and red hair. She had this incredible air of innocence about her that made him want to protect her from the world. Jackson hadn't experienced that in a woman in a very long time. Most of the women he dealt with were professionals, hardened by their work, be it on the street or off. He felt ready for someone a little, well, vulnerable. Not so suspicious of everyone and everything. Willing to accept.

Man, he thought, *she is so small*; he felt huge beside her, the same way Marvin had stated she made him feel. He could break her in two if he wanted. Ah, but he didn't. What he did want was to take her to bed, make slow, tender love with her. Show her his power, yet in a subtle way. He wondered if she wanted him as badly as he did her. He wondered if she felt the chemistry as he did.

Gillian came back carrying mugs, startling him out of his thoughts. "I thought coffee might go well," she said, handing one to him.

Jack nodded his head, agreeing.

She sat on the other end of the couch from him. He smiled slightly as she sank into the billowy softness. He watched as she sat her mug down on the coffee table, removed her shoes, lifted up slightly, placing her feet under her, turning to him.

"So," she said.

"So," he said.

They looked at each other.

"I've never done this before," Gillian whispered.

He cocked his head, not sure what she meant.

"Meeting someone for the first time and all and not even having a real first date, actually, I've never wanted to – it always takes me awhile before I feel the attraction, the chemistry, the need, I guess."

He waited.

"It's different with you," she said, glancing away embarrassedly.

He was intrigued by her lack of boldness, her almost childlike shyness with him. He wanted her badly.

He waited for her to bring her eyes back to his, then said, his voice husky, "Come here."

She slowly rose, walked to him, stood before him.

"It's different with you, too," he said, his voice strained.

She smiled at this, reached down, took his hand, led him to the bedroom.

Breaking away, Gillian went to the nightstand, turned on a small, white boudoir lamp, illuminating a small portion of the room. Jack took note of all the whiteness in here, too, but only cognitively; his attention was riveted to her. She stood by the bed, watching him, giving the impression of an awkwardness within herself, as if she wasn't sure what to do now.

He went toward her, took her in his arms, once more aware of how much larger than her he was, lifting her up slightly, bending his head down as she tilted hers up, their lips coming together.

She moaned lowly as he kissed her, as if deeply content to be there in his arms. He eventually picked her up, laying her on the bed, lying beside her, and his mouth on hers, began to remove her clothes, seeing her with his hands as her clothing was slowly removed.

She docilely let him undress her, her hands on his face, in his hair, on his neck, her mouth lingering heatedly on his.

He finally pulled his head away, raised up, in order to slide her panties down her legs, staring at her naked form.

She was small, almost like a child, the only proof of her maturity being her round, firm breasts. The copper-colored triangle between her legs he expected to see was not there. He reached out, touched her, ran his hand over the smoothness, then looked at her.

"I shave there," she said, acting embarrassed. "In college, this guy I was dating gave me scabies. It was an awful experience. Ever since,

I don't feel clean unless I shave there, you know, making sure." She shrugged. He moved his hand over her skin again, studying her, realizing it was a turn-on for him, the exposure of her outer sex.

He moved his mouth to that area, felt her stiffen as his tongue caressed, then heard her loud sigh of contentment, could feel her body relaxing as he made love to her with his mouth.

She eventually reached down, put her hands on his face, drew him up to her.

"Your turn," she murmured, gently maneuvering him on his back.

"Well, if you insist," he drawled.

She smiled, her hands going to his shirt. Undressed him slowly, her mouth trailing her hands.

He found himself sighing contentedly as her mouth caressed his body.

"You're so beautiful," she murmured, her tongue traveling down his abdomen, sighing as she reached her destination, taking hold with her mouth.

After awhile, he pulled her into his arms, said, "Gillian, I don't have a condom. Jeez, I'm sorry, I didn't even think about it but I'm clean, no disease of any sort, I swear."

"Hey, Jackson, you think I would have asked you into my abode if I thought there was any chance of that?" she asked, her mouth lingering at the base of his throat. "And just so you know," she said, her mouth traveling again, "I'm clean too, was just tested last month, in fact, no problem."

"No way," he said, stopping her progress, pulling her up to him, then rolling her on her back, hovering over her. "My turn now," he said, pinning her with his body, placing his mouth on her neck, beginning his own journey.

She was passive, compliant as he loved her body, not as energetic as other women he had known, not as involved. He hoped to bring her to climax with his hands and mouth, as she had him. He moved back to her mouth, caressing her supple body with his hands.

"Now, Jackson," she whispered, arching her hips, offering herself to him, pulling him toward her, "love me now."

He entered her, hearing her hiss as he penetrated, began moving within her. She moved her hips as he thrust, working herself, a thin sheaf of perspiration coating her body. He forced himself to slow down, waiting for her to climax. She seemed to become frantic with her movements, laboring her body, and he realized with some frustration what she was trying to attain.

He stopped, put his face close to hers, whispered, "Let me do it," as he rode her, trying not to achieve his own orgasm, waiting for her. She gasped, held fast to his back, and not sure whether she had climaxed or not, unable to hold himself back any longer, he pounded himself into her, hoping he had brought her the sweet release she had brought him twice now.

Afterward, he rolled off her, onto his back, staring at the ceiling, sweat coursing off his body, breathing heavily, waiting for his heart and respiration to slow, waiting till he could talk and be understood.

He turned his head, looked at her. Her eyes were closed, her breathing was shallow, slow. She was slightly flushed. Beads of perspiration stood out on her forehead, upper lip. She had a calm, serene look on her face. A look which he knew had to belie what her body must be feeling.

She seemed to feel him watching, opened her eyes, rolled her head toward his. He cocked his head slightly, studying her.

As if reading the question on his mind, she said, her voice low, "Please don't blame yourself because I couldn't – I didn't – it's not your fault. It's me, it comes from me, from something I don't want to talk about. I just can't. I've never been able to. I pushed us tonight because what I feel for you is so, well, forceful. I thought maybe – but understand, Jack, if you had been any other man, I would have faked it, acted like I had, but I couldn't do that, not with you. You're different, you're special. I want what we have to be honest, without lies or deceits, and that's why I didn't . . ."

He put his fingers to her mouth, hushing her, saw the tears come to her eyes.

"I'm sorry," he said.

She took hold of his hand, moving her mouth from his pressing fingers to the palm, lingering there, then drew it away, said, "Just please don't be the type of man who has to prove his virility through your partner's climax. Please, Jack, don't be like that. It has nothing to do with you. It's me. It's my problem."

He rolled onto his side, stroked her shoulder, watched her shiver in response, whispered, "It's our problem now and something we can at least work on, don't you think?"

She studied his eyes, then gave him a shy smile. "I knew you were different," she said, going into his arms.

CHAPTER 11

The man lays sprawled on the bed, the woman straddling him. She moves her body slowly, rotating her hips, occasionally lifting up, leaning forward, then backwards, building friction. His eyes are closed, his body sweating, his breathing heavy. She watches his face, waiting. Her body aches. She has allowed him to play out his favorite fantasy with her and he has been harsh but she does not mind; his reward is coming soon.

She moves her throbbing body, increasing speed, patient with his endurance. He grasps her hips, pulling her onto him harder, his head thrown back, his mouth forming a grimace.

After his movements have quieted, she removes his hands from her body, places each one above his head, and using the leather straps he has utilized with her earlier, ties each hand to the bedpost, making sure to knot the straps twice.

He opens his eyes. She smiles at him, murmurs to him, kissing his eyes closed. He smiles back, anticipating what she intends to do with him, closing his eyes, waiting.

She raises up, as if stretching, carefully reaches up under the wig, at the back of her head, removes the long, sharply pointed piece of steel, watching, making sure his eyes don't open suddenly, placing the middle finger of her right hand in the loop at the end. With her left hand, she tenderly traces his ribs, counting up, stopping at the fifth rib, resting her fingers on the sternum. Using her right hand, she quickly inserts the pin deep into the tender area directly beside her left hand, forcing it with the palms of both hands now, twisting it several times.

His heart begins to leak immediately. He opens his eyes, wide with terror. She smiles tenderly at him, placing her hand on his face, stroking. He begins to struggle, but is already weak, his life ending as his heart stops. "Goodbye Wayne," the woman whispers, her voice low, leaning down into his face, staring at him intently, watching the light begin to fade from his eyes.

Then hurrying, knowing there is not much time left before the blood will stop flowing, she lifts herself off him, gets up off the bed, runs to the bathroom, removes the condom she had inserted, flushes it down the toilet.

She then returns to the bedroom area, retrieves her tote satchel, goes back to the bathroom, placing the satchel on the back of the toilet. Reaching inside, she removes a scalpel from a hidden compartment in the bottom, returns to the dead man, and sets to work.

When she has finished, leaning over him, she kisses him fully on the lips, then whispers, her mouth against his, "I love you, Daddy."

Making sure not to step or place her hands onto any part of the bed or carpet containing blood, so as not to leave any prints, she goes into the bathroom, throws the scalpel and steel pin into the sink, turns on the shower as hot as she can get it. She rinses the blood from her hands in the sink, then sticks her mouth under the faucet, greedily gulping water, her mouth dry from the antihistamines she has taken earlier.

She reaches into the satchel, pulls out incense and a lighter, places the stick of incense on the back of the toilet, lights it, breathes in the sweet cinnamon smell as she removes the wig, tossing it and the lighter into her satchel.

After making sure her hair is tucked in tight beneath the skull cap, she steps into the tub, not bothering to draw the shower curtain. She lets the water course over her body, sluicing the blood away. She checks the tips of her fingers, satisfied they are still dehydrated from the medication.

She has shaved her pubis, legs, and beneath her arms that morning but runs her hands over her body again, assuring herself once more there is no pertinent hair anywhere that would be detected if the police are smart enough to check.

She relays in her mind what they had done before the act. She had refused anything to eat or drink, acting eager to play their game. Has she touched anything with her hands? Only him and surely a palm print could not be traced to her. She will check the bedroom again before she leaves to make sure there are no footprints from her. Her hands go to the scalp cap once more, making sure there are no stray hairs that will be washed away in case any eager-beaver homicide technician decides to pull the drain.

She takes the small packaged bar of soap, peels the paper off, throws it in the toilet, then begins to wash her body with her hands. When she is finished, she turns the shower off, stands there a moment, letting the water run from her body, letting the air dry her.

She reaches out, grabs a hand towel, wipes the shower faucet and handle off, then throws it on the floor, stepping onto it. Retrieves another one, toweling herself off with that. When she is finished, she takes the soap from the shower, wraps it in a tissue, puts it into her satchel, then flushes the toilet, watching the paper that had contained the soap spiral down.

She turns to the sink, rinses the soap off her hands, and with the water still running, carefully washes off the scalpel and pin with her fingers, placing them in the hidden section in the bottom of her satchel when she is finished, along with the wig and butane lighter.

She wipes down the counter and sink and the handle to the toilet with a dry washcloth, then bends down, picking up the towel off the floor, and stuffs the washcloth and two hand towels into her hidden compartment.

She snuffs out the tip of the incense with her fingers, throws the remainder of the wand down the toilet, flushes it again, her fingers swathed in tissue paper.

She walks into the bedroom naked, goes and stands in front of the dresser, surveying her body in the mirror, turning this way and that. She studies herself, sure she will be bruised from his assault, then goes to her clothes which she had made sure would be far enough away from the bed to avoid any spraying, and dresses herself, watching the man the whole time.

When she is finished, her eyes survey the room, lingering on the wall behind the bed, ticking off items, making sure nothing will be left behind.

She has checked the bathroom before she left it; the condom is gone, the towels in her satchel along with the victim's billfold which she removed from his pants pocket with one of the towels wrapped around her hand. There are no glasses with her prints on it. She has not stepped in any blood.

Finally satisfied that there are no clues left behind and the room is clean of any residue from her body, she goes to the door, peeking out. There is no one in the hallway, so she steps out, making sure to use the sleeve of her coat to cover her hand as she turns the handle, then stands there, removing the skull cap, which she also places into the secret compartment of her satchel. She shakes her hair out, letting it settle down her back, settles the satchel on her shoulder, then goes to the elevator.

She is not the same woman who came in with the man in room 506.

CHAPTER 12

The man's nude body lay sprawled on his back on the bed. This scene could have been a repeat of the first except the victim's hands had been tied to the headboard with leather straps. Jack knew before allowing his eyes to follow the trail that the words on the wall above the bed would say, "Wayne's Dead."

"Who the hell is this Wayne anyway?" Jack asked no one in particular.

Bogie looked up from placing a blood-soaked Q-tip into a paper envelope. "I think your perp is trying to kill Wayne, whoever he is, over and over again, for whatever reason." He shrugged, pulling out another cotton swab. "If you ask me, ole Wayne must have done somebody some pretty heavy damage at one time or another."

"You into psychology now, Boge?" Marvin asked, grinning.

"You got a better explanation?" Bogie said, removing his rubber gloves, donning another pair.

"Makes sense to me," Jack said, staring at the bloody corpse.

"Looks like we got us one perverted killer on our hands," Marvin said. "Wonder what we'll find at the next one."

Jack looked at him. "You thinking this is serial?"

"Don't it look like it to you?" Marvin responded.

"Let's just pray there's not gonna be a next scene," Jack said.

"I think you're gonna be disappointed," Bogie said, taking out a paper bag.

"Shit," Jack said, his voice low.

"Still think your killer's a male, Jack?" Bogie asked.

Jack nodded his head.

"I disagree," Bogie said, his voice mild.

"Man, look at all this blood," Marvin said. "You trying to tell me a woman did this kind of damage?"

Bogie shook his head yes.

"Naw, man, I think Jack's right. It's gotta be a man done this. Women don't usually get this violent or this bloody. They don't cut off men's body parts – " then stopped, thinking.

Bogie lifted his eyebrows.

"Okay, okay, maybe some do. But you're saying there's some woman out there, going around, screwing these guys, then killing them and cutting their nuts off? Man, that hurts." His hand went toward his crotch, causing Jack to grin.

"Marvin," Bogie intoned, his voice sonorous, "I would advise you to keep it where it belongs till we find this killer. I wouldn't want to come upon you some fine day lying on a hotel bed, your left nut on the floor." Everyone laughed.

"We'll need to do an NCIC BOLO," Jack thought aloud. "See if any other city has had any similar type murder."

Robin, who had been quietly studying the scene spoke up. "I'll take care of that as soon as I get back to the station."

"My bet would be you'll get some feedback," Bogie interjected. "I don't think these are the first two killings this person has done, if you want my opinion. Too clean, too well-organized."

Marvin said, "You know what that means? We got to deal with the Feebs. Damn."

"They're not so bad," Bogie said, grinning widely.

"It's been, what, since the last killing," Jack said, "four weeks, five?"

"More like six," Marvin said. He studied Jack. "Why?"

"Aren't women more cyclic than men?" Jack asked, looking at Bogie. "You know, the PMS factor, that sort of thing?"

Bogie thought a moment. "I don't think there's enough known about serial killers to establish that, especially women serial killers," he finally said. "In any event, six weeks rules that out, but I still say it's a member of the female gender, for whatever that's worth."

"Hey, maybe the dude doing the killing is named Wayne," Marvin said, his eyes gleaming, staring at the blood-spattered wall.

They all looked at him.

"Now, don't go lookin' at me like I'm out in the ozone somewhere," Marvin said defensively. "Just listen to what I'm sayin'."

"Certainly, Marvin, why don't you enlighten us on your unspoken theory," Jack said.

"That man has got an attitude problem that won't quit," Marvin said to Bogie. "Shit, man, you don't know what I have to endure, putting up with his crap all the damn day long. Hey, I didn't join the police force to have to put up with harassment coming from no white man, you hear?" he asked, causing Jack and Bogie to laugh.

After everyone had sobered, Marvin went on. "What I was saying is maybe Wayne is the name of the killer. How many serial killers are there anyway with the name Wayne? Well, let's see. Wayne Williams, John Wayne Gacy, Jeffrey DeWayne Dahmer . . ."

"I don't think his middle name was DeWayne," Jack cut in.

"You sure? Well, we can always find that out. But just look at it, why don't you? Seems an awful lot of them buggers have the same name. Maybe we got us a serial killer wannabe here, trying to take that name. What you say?"

Jack and Bogie looked at each other. "You never know," Jack finally said, shrugging.

"I'm sticking with a woman," Bogie said, going back to work, turning his back on the two.

"Whatever, just consider it, okay?" Marvin asked. "Ain't gonna hurt anything, you consider my theory."

"Never said it wouldn't," Jack said, heading toward the door. "Well, come on, Marvelous Marv, let's go see if we can find out from the desk clerk if anyone happens to know this guy."

"Bet you ten to one, he signed in as John Wayne," Marvin said, following along behind.

In the elevator, Jack whistled a tune under his breath. Marvin studied him, then said. "Man, I been worried about you."

Jack looked at him.

"For the past few weeks, you ain't been acting like yourself," he observed.

Jack stayed silent.

"Used to go ranting and raving around, acting all sullified and hateful to everybody. But lately, you been acting more, well, happy sure ain't the word for you, but it's close enough, I guess. Although you do still backslide every once in a while."

Jack smiled at him.

"Yeah, that's it right there. You hardly used to smile before. Now I catch you doing it all the time. You care to tell me what's going on with you?"

"Nothing," Jack said, facing the front of the elevator.

Marvin watched him, then, "Oh, I get it. I know what it is. Old

Jack Daniels done gone and found hisself a main squeeze, somebody he can release his pent-up energy on, somebody to tame down that testosterone level a little bit, make the guy act more like a human being, one of the species."

Jack ignored him.

"Well, you gonna tell me who she is?" Marvin demanded. "Shoot, man, I'm your best pal in the whole, wide world, you at least ought to confide in me every once in a while. Make me feel special, you know."

Jack continued to ignore his friend.

The elevator stopped, the doors slid open. Marvin stepped forward, turned, and blocked Jack from exiting.

Their eyes met. "The cat woman," Jack said, grinning widely, then stepped around Marvin.

"Say what?" Marvin asked, his voice rising an octave. Jack grinned wider. Marvin caught up with him. "The cat woman, as in my cat woman?" Marvin asked him.

"None other," Jack said.

Marvin put his hand out, grabbing Jack's arm, stopping him.

They looked at each other. "Now don't go getting territorial on me," Jack said, reading his look. "You're married, remember? Gillian's single, so am I. I know you found her attractive, well, so did I when I met her."

"Oh, you talking about that day she came looking for me and you talked to her instead."

"Right, and we've been seeing each other ever since." Jack smiled again.

"Shit man, I liked you better hateful and ugly," Marvin said, turning and going toward the reservations desk.

They studied the admittance card. "What'd I tell you?" Marvin asked, pointing. "John Wayne." They looked at each other.

"It's a woman," Marvin said. "Has to be."

"Yeah, and just what makes you think that?"

"A woman, a romantic rendezvous, interlude, whatever you might wish to call it, my man, in essence, the guy's fuck, would maybe think it was funny having him sign in as John Wayne. You know? Think it's cute. A joke between the two. Can't see two men doing that, can you? I mean, a man talking another man into signing in as

John Wayne."

"Unless it's some sort of code or something," Jack said, studying the card. He shook his head. "Not the same handwriting as the other, so our perp isn't signing for them, looks like." He turned to Marvin. "We ever get a sample of the first victim's handwriting? I never saw that report if we did."

Marvin nodded. "Yep, the dude signed himself in, according to his grieving widow."

"We'll need to compare this one's handwriting, too, see if he signed the register or someone else did for him."

Marvin nodded in agreement, then, "Still need to do the fingerprints," he said, indicating the card, "although probably be like the other, give us nothing but the victim's and hotel clerk's along with a bunch of smudges."

Jack nodded his head. He looked at Marvin. "What about two guys agree to meet at the hotel, for whatever reason . . ."

"The reason was to fuck, my man, go look at the condom still hanging off that dead guy's dick."

"Whatever," Jack said. "So the guy signing in just tells the other guy to ask for the room of John Wayne. An easy enough name to remember, wouldn't you say?"

Marvin considered this. "Well, yeah, I 'spose. But I got to tell you, I'm starting to side with Bogie on this. It feels like a woman thing to me."

"Notice anything else?" Jack asked.

Marvin studied the card. "Gave his address as the courthouse, just like the first one."

Jack nodded his head.

"Shit," Marvin said, studying the card.

Jack shrugged his shoulders, looking around. "Well, let's do our job, guy. You talk to the security guard, I'll interview the manager, get all the info we need."

"Man, this is getting old already," Marvin said in a whiny tone.

"Yeah, well, just wait till the feebs start in," Jack warned.

Jack was late for the protocol meeting that afternoon, having stopped by Gillian's apartment for lunch which they never got around to. When he walked in, there were two new faces sitting at the conference table, stone-faced, watching everyone else watch them. Jack sighed inwardly, but at the same time felt relief it was these two. They were notorious for watching an investigation but actually never entering it unless a superior was involved. Then they got involved. Or if the case was cracked, they always took the credit.

"Well, I see the feds made it," Jack said, his voice mild, belying the irritation he felt.

McKinley nodded his head, waving for Jack to sit down. "I believe everyone here knows Peters and Burks." No one acknowledged, almost everyone with grim expressions on their faces.

Jack sneaked a glance at Bogie, who was grinning, seeming happy at this. Jack suspected Bogie liked to sit back and watch the interactions between people, getting a kick out of all the internal battles going on, always seeming to stay friends with everyone, sitting on the sidelines, detached from all the in-house fighting.

"Okay," McKinley said, drawing attention back to himself. "I've briefed Peters and Burks on what we've got so far."

Everyone turned to the two federal agents. Burks, a short, squat, rotund man with a round face and protruding front teeth, who Jack thought resembled a beaver greatly, leaned forward, giving them an intense look. "We've decided to step back on the investigation at this point," he said. Jack could feel the tenseness in the air fade a little. "We'll expect to see all the reports, be kept informed step by step. If we feel the investigation should be done differently, we'll let you know. If we feel more needs to be done, you can count on hearing from us. And, of course, if you need our help, we'll be more than happy to step in."

"What about profiling this killer for us?" Robin asked, looking annoyed. "Can't you at least have that done?"

The two agents exchanged a look. "Honey, we got to fill out a thirty to forty page report, then send it on to Quantico," Peters said. "Our profilers are so backed up now, it'll be next year before they can get to this one, so what's the hurry?" giving Robin a grin.

"My name's Robin, not honey," she snapped. Then, exasperatedly, "My God, NCIC is starting to spit out killings similar to this all over the Southeast for the past twelve years, and you're just going to let this slide?" Neither one responded, both looking bored. "So, exactly why are you here then, you're not going to get involved, you're not going to do anything?" she asked, growing angry. "I mean, what do we need you two jerks for?"

Marvin grinned. Jack and Bogie glanced at each other.

"Okay, okay," McKinley interrupted, seeing the two agents' faces going red, half-afraid they'd change their minds and decide to join the investigation. "Let's not get our panties in a bind," he said, looking at Robin, sending her a message with his eyes.

She immediately backed down, leaned back in her seat, crossed her arms.

The sergeant sighed, then turned desperate eyes to Bogie. "What about it, Boge? You get anything this morning?"

Bogie shrugged. "Not so far, no," he said, looking forlorn, "but I haven't gone through everything yet. Besides, she's going to slip sometime, she can't perform a perfect killing each and every time."

"I still don't see how a woman can be doing this," Jack said, leaning toward him.

"I guess time will tell," McKinley said. "Okay, we got an ID on this one?" looking at everyone in turn.

No one answered.

"Well, I guess we got us some footwork to do," he said, rising from the table. "Burks, Peters, good to see you, and we'll give you everything we've got so you can get that report filed. You guys," looking at Jack and the others, "do your thing. I want to know who this guy is by this p.m."

Jack and Marvin stayed behind the others. They looked at each other. "You get the security tape yet?" Marvin asked.

Jack nodded.

Marvin thought. "Okay, we checked the first one together, let's do this one separate. See if anyone on the second looks familiar to anyone on the first."

Jack nodded, thinking. "You know there's not much chance we'll actually see the same two people."

"Yeah, but you never know, guy," Marvin said. "Stranger things have happened before."

Jack snorted.

"I figured we'd get together at lunch and compare notes," Marvin said, sounding irritated.

Jack looked at him, then shrugged. "I met Gillian. Sorry, I didn't think." He leaned back. "You get anything?"

Marvin shook his head. "Same old, same old, nobody saw anything or anybody."

"I might have something," Jack said. "I talked to the guy who signed the deceased in. He remembered the John Wayne thing. Thought it was some guy getting something on the side, you know, not wanting his wife or anyone he might know to find out. Said he paid in cash."

"Sounds logical," Marvin agreed. "Did he have anybody with him?"

"He said no, but about ten minutes later, this woman in a trench coat and dark hair wearing sunglasses at night," Jack paused long enough to raise his eyebrows at this, "came into the lobby and went straight upstairs. Didn't sign in, didn't ask for anyone's room number. He figures she might have been with the victim."

"Makes sense," Marvin said. "He don't want to be recognized, neither does she, except she probably called all kinds of attention to herself wearing sunglasses at night and indoors."

"Right," Jack said, leaning forward. "So, the way I see it, that rules her out right off. If she's our killer, she wouldn't want anyone to see her and remember her, so she sure as hell wouldn't wear shades at night and inside."

Marvin nodded, thinking, then straightened up. "Except, if this is our killer and she's got balls the size of Seattle or maybe is playing with us, what better way? Disguise herself, wear the sunglasses, strut right on past the video camera, daring us to notice her."

Jack stiffened. "Wait a minute, didn't we see a woman with dark hair wearing a trench coat in the other security film?"

Marvin snapped his fingers. "Man, you're right, just for a second, as she went by."

"Yeah, her back to the camera," Jack agreed. They looked at each other. "Maybe we'll get a face view this time," he said, rising.

They watched the second video together, found the woman right off, although the camera caught her peripherally as she went by the registration desk, almost out of range, giving them just a glimpse of dark hair and a trench coat. The way her face was turned, they couldn't see her sunglasses.

"Same hairdo as the first one," Marvin observed.

"This can't be coincidence," Jack said.

"I don't know, man, there's a lot of dark-headed women out there, and both nights, it was rainy and cool."

Jack rewound the tape, watched it again.

Robin opened the door, came in, sat down beside Marvin, said, "Well, we've got the ID."

"Wait, let me guess, another lawyer, right?" Marvin asked before she could relay anything.

"Yep. One Mr. Sanford Goeller, white male, age 48, partner with the most esteemed firm of Goeller and Goeller, the other Goeller being his wife."

"Uh-oh," Marvin said.

Robin looked at Jack. "You want me to talk to the widow?" she asked.

He thought a minute. "Yeah, that's probably a good idea, after the way I flubbed it up with Ms. Walters." He looked at her. "One thing, Robin, as delicately as you can, see if she knew or suspected hubby might have been interested in his own gender, might have been into something on the side."

"Whew, that's gonna be hard to put delicately," Robin said.

Marvin laughed. "Yeah, Jack found that out the hard way," he said.

"Bogie figured out what the killing instrument is yet?" she asked.

Jack shrugged. "All he can determine so far is it's small, cylindrical, and pointed at the end." He looked at them. "That's why I say it can't be a woman doing this. That takes a lot of strength, pushing something like that into a man's chest, without him fighting or knocking the killer off. Much less hiding it."

"Well, yeah, but it looks like they're distracted when it happens," Robin said.

"Yeah, man, after you just finished spilling your gism into some woman, how you feeling?" Marvin asked. "You looking around, observing everything going on around you, you already getting up and leaving? Most men, the thing they'd most like to do in the world is turn over and go to sleep. They ain't even thinking about having to fight off some woman wanting to pierce their heart and then slice off their nut."

"That, gentlemen, is what I would call a rude awakening," Robin said, getting up and leaving, their laughter trailing her.

After they had sobered, Jack looked at Marvin. "You know what this means?"

Marvin shook his head forlornly. "Yeah, man, we got to watch this entire tape, see when the woman in the trench coat left."

"If she left by the front entrance," Jack said, knowing chances were, she didn't.

CHAPTER 13

Sanford Goeller's widow agreed to meet with them after hours at the law offices of Goeller and Goeller. Jack and Marvin walked into an ornately decorated reception area, all dark woods and carpets with wainscoting and English hunt paintings on the walls.

"Whooee, man, take a gander at this," Marvin said, looking around.

"Another rich attorney," Jack said, searching for the receptionist.

Marvin gave Jack a warning look. "Don't get me started," he said, causing Jack to grin.

A forty-ish looking woman entered the room, acting as if she knew they were there. Jack suspected some sort of signaling or video device.

She came toward them, held her hand out. "I'm Sandra Goeller," she said, shaking hands with each one of them as they introduced themselves.

Jack studied her, noticing the puffy eyes, reddened nose. She was dressed in a black business suit and was short with a slender build.

"Can we do this in my office?" she asked them.

They followed her down a narrow hall, their feet falling silently on the thick carpeting.

Widow Goeller escorted them into a corner office, the view offering a silvery slice of the Tennessee River behind her desk. She sat down in an executive chair, indicating with a wave for them to sit in two wingback chairs across from her.

After they were seated, she said, "What can I do for you, gentlemen?" her voice soft, Southern.

Marvin started off by saying, "We're sorry for the loss of your husband, Ms. Goeller, but we need to go over a few things with you."

Her eyes watered slightly, but she blinked, clearing them, then said, "Of course, anything I can do to help."

"Ms. Goeller, we read the initial interview with one of our detectives and would like to expand on a few matters," Jack said, waited for her nod of acceptance, then, "I was wondering if your husband had been known to be gone from home overnight on a frequent basis?"

She studied him, then said, "You're wondering if I knew he was having an affair."

Jack straightened at that.

"Mr. Daniels, I was married to that man for twenty-five years," she said, her voice low. "We were committed to each other. I still cannot accept his death as it was. No, Sandy was not having an affair. He was never away from home overnight." She paused. "Except for that night," she finished, then sat there, breathing deeply. Tears were running down her face. "We loved each other," she finally said, her voice breaking.

Jack and Marvin waited uncomfortably as she dabbed at the tears on her face, then snatched a tissue from the holder on her desk and blew her nose.

"Do you know how he happened to be at that hotel on that particular night, then?" Jack asked, making his voice as gentle as he could.

She chewed her bottom lip, blinking severely to stop the flow of tears. "He had been to depositions that afternoon. We had planned to go out to dinner that evening, then maybe a movie, you know, do something relaxing, but Sandy called at five, said something had come up with his client during the depositions and he needed to meet with him that evening to clear the discrepancy up."

"What discrepancy was that," Jack asked, "if I may ask?"

"I'm sorry, attorney-client privilege. Sandy wouldn't have even been able to tell me himself."

"And you took him at his word?" Marvin asked.

She sniffled. "Of course. Sandy didn't lie to me. We never lied to each other." She began to cry heavily. "We loved each other!" she said, almost defensively.

They waited her out.

"Do you know who the client was?" Jack asked, when she had calmed down.

"Yes, I checked his appointment book after I – after it – when the other detective was here. The client was Norman March. I talked to him later, but he said that nothing had happened during the deposition to raise any questions and that Sandy hadn't needed to talk to him afterwards." She gave them a confused look. "I can't believe he would have just lied to me about something like that," she said. "It wasn't like Sandy to do that."

Jack and Marvin nodded in unison.

"Ma'am, have you thought of anyone other than the names you gave the detective that your husband might have seen or had contact with the day of his death?" Jack asked.

Ms. Goeller shook her head no.

Jack nodded, aware that the names she had given them had all been checked out and alibied.

"Have you thought of anyone who might have felt animosity toward your husband?" Marvin asked.

She shook her head adamantly. "Sandy was a very popular man," she said. "Very well-liked. Very civic-minded, an avid church-goer, very much involved with community life. I know of no one that had any ill feelings at all toward him."

"Ma'am, I'm sorry to ask this, but had your husband had an affair before, that you're aware of?" Marvin asked.

She emphatically shook her head no.

"Had he ever called and told you he would be late like he did that night?" Marvin pushed.

She shook her head adamantly. "No, never. We were always together. Even when he went out of town, we went together, if possible. We were close, officers. I don't know if I can stress that enough, but we had a good marriage. We just didn't do things like that to each other."

Jack and Marvin nodded their heads consolingly.

She wrung her hands together. "I've just buried my best friend," she said, looking lost. "How could this have happened? What in the world was he doing in that hotel room?"

"I'm sorry, Ms. Goeller," Jack said, feeling it.

He glanced at Marvin, saw Marvin was going to make him be the bad guy.

"Ms. Goeller, I apologize, but I need to ask this question."

"No, it's all right," she said, sniffling. "Go ahead, ask whatever you need to."

"Ma'am, did your husband have any unusual sexual interests that you're aware of?"

"Meaning?" she asked, giving him a sharp look.

Jack hesitated. "Well, bondage and discipline, sadomasochism, anything like that?"

She gave him a shocked look. "No, of course not. He was, I guess, a very ordinary, normal man."

"What about sex with a male partner? Did he ever show any interest in that, that you're aware of?"

She seemed to gasp. "Of course not." She looked from Jack to Marvin, then back to Jack. "Have I not been told everything here? Are you saying Sandy was with another man? That just couldn't be. Sandy was not a homosexual."

She stopped, studying their faces.

"Was there anything unusual at the scene of his murder you're not telling me?" she asked.

"We're just trying to explore every possibility here," Jack said. "I don't mean to indicate that your husband was with another man, Ms. Goeller. We don't know what happened. That's why I'm asking these terrible questions."

She seemed to calm, then said, "Mr. Daniels, my husband was a very loving, caring man. He was tender, very gentle. We were good together, if you understand what I mean. We were very much in love. We had a normal, healthy sexual relationship. I would never have suspected Sandy of anything other than heterosexual activity. Ever." She stopped, then, "Or of having sex with anyone but me," she added, then began crying again.

They waited uncomfortably.

After she had calmed, Jack leaned toward her and his voice as gentle as he could make it, asked, "Ms. Goeller, this will sound very strange to you, but did your husband ever go by another name other than his given one?"

She looked at them. "Just Sandy mostly, his nickname for Sanford. He didn't have a middle name."

Jack nodded.

"We were together for twenty-five years," she continued, dabbing at her eyes. "I know it's different with men, the sex thing, but I thought I was all he needed, I thought I gave him all he needed. Now, I wonder. He's left me here to wonder about that for the rest of my life."

She looked at them. Jack was finding it difficult to meet her gaze.

"Please find out what happened to him. Please solve this case and find out why he was there. Please." She gave them a pitiful look. "Our son's been away at college. He's home now. How do I explain this to him?" she asked them. "How do I make him understand when I can't understand?"

She was still crying when they left, feeling like lowlifes slinking out of those ornate offices.

They were silent most of the way back to the station. After stopping the car, Jack looked at Marvin.

Marvin shook his head. "No way that woman killed her old man," he said, his voice low. "Did you see how upset she was? She could hardly talk to us for all the crying she was doing."

Jack nodded, thinking. "Yeah, but to be a good lawyer, don't you have to be a good actor?"

"You think all that could have just been an act? Maybe she found out he was having an affair, maybe she . . ." Marvin started.

"She was home alone the night of the murder," Jack said.

"No alibi at all," Marvin said. "Maybe all those tears are from guilt, remorse for offing her husband."

"Could be, man, but we're forgetting something," Jack interrupted. "He was killed like the other one, exact same MO. I doubt she had any kind of connection to Walters."

"I been thinking about that," Marvin said.

Jack looked at him.

"Maybe there's some kind of wive's club out there," Marvin continued. "Maybe these women find out their old man's screwing around on them, there's a number they can call, someone who will take care of it for them."

"You serious?" Jack asked.

Marvin sighed. "No, man, just throwing out everything I can think of, hoping to hit on something. There was a movie, you know, about these white bitches, their husbands all divorced them for these nice, cute, little other white bitches, and they decided to get them back."

"Yeah, but in a passive way," Jack said.

"Well, sure," Marvin said, "but look at it this way. Wouldn't you say, among the professions, that lawyers are about the world's worst sort of people, generally speaking? Not well-respected, you know that, and wasn't there a survey a while back about the professions most prone for adultery and that included lawyers and preachers and I forget what the third group was."

"Yeah, I remember that."

"Okay, so these lawyers' wives got some sort of secret club they belong to, and when ole hubby starts fooling around, planting the salami where it don't need to be planted, maybe this club provides a service. Them women don't want to divorce their dudes. Look at all the money these guys have, they don't want to lose that. So, what's a better way of putting a stop to the old fart's philandering? Huh? Get the club's killer to put a stop to the old man hisself. You get left with the estate, all kinds of money to play with, maybe buy you a big old piece of candy you can play with anytime you want, and who's gonna stop you?"

Jack grinned. "Marvin, my man, you have got one imagination on you," he said.

"Hey, stranger things have happened," Marvin said.

"Ain't that the truth," Jack agreed.

Jack started to open his door, then stopped. "Okay, six weeks since the first one. Wonder how long our killer's gonna give us till the next one?"

They looked at each other.

"If this is a serial killer," Marvin mused, "don't they usually want to be caught? Don't they usually leave clues around, signs pointing to them?"

"Eventually, I guess," Jack answered. "Only thing we got so far is the name Wayne, and that may just tie into the name the victim signs in under and nothing else." He thought a minute. "Don't they usually get caught up in the publicity their killings get?" he asked, turning to Marvin. "Isn't that a big thing with them?"

"I know it was for the Son of Sam," Marvin said, thinking. "But you know what McKinley said, try not to let the media get hold of this or else there's gonna be mass panic."

"Yeah, but how do you keep something like this from getting out, man? Too many people know about it already."

"Well, I know one person won't be talking."

"Who's that?"

"Ms. Goeller. You think she wants the whole world to know her husband was found sprawled on a bed, his wrists tied to the headboard, naked as the day he was born, a condom on his cold penis, his left testicle cut off?"

When they got back to the station, Bogie was waiting on them.
"We got something!" Bogie said as they walked toward him.
Jack, catching his excitement, said, "Yeah? Thank God. What?"
"A long, black hair."
"Matches the woman we've seen on the tapes," Marvin said, musing.
"The bad part is, the hair is from a wig, not an actual person's scalp," Bogie replied.
"Wig? You mean a synthetic hair?" Jack asked.
"No, my man, I mean a dead human hair made into a wig."
"How do you know that?" Marvin asked.
"No root on the end, boy-o. Whoever killed them is wearing a real human hair wig, black in color."
"It's got to be that woman on the tapes," Marvin said.
"Told you it was a woman," Bogie said smugly.
Jackson thought.
"Maybe not."
Marvin looked at him. "Huh?"
"Could be a transvestite," he said, thinking. "Man dressed like a woman, wearing a wig. We all know the most vicious killers are homosexuals and the two victims we have so far, by all accounts, were heterosexual. That could be a way to lure them into the hotel room, you know, a man dressed like a woman, a transvestite."
"But the person on those tapes looks like a woman," Marvin said. "Looks small in frame, you know."
"How can you tell with that trench coat on?" Jack asked. "That could hide a heavier framed man trying to pass as a woman."
"It's hard to tell from the tapes, but she looks to have a small face."
"How can you tell the way her face is turned in both the videos? All we got at most is a side profile and a slight one at that."
They stood there thinking.
"Besides," Jack finally said, "it could have just been a coincidence she was even there both those nights."

"In my business, there is no such thing as coincidence," Bogie intoned.

"Not to mention, she wasn't caught on either tape leaving the building," Marvin said. "That makes her all the more suspect, you ask me."

Jack was shaking his head with frustration.

"Can we trace the wig?" Marvin asked Bogie.

"Who knows?" Bogie answered. "My guess is the killer purchased it long before she came to Knoxville. How many other cities we got the same kind of killings in?"

"All over the friggin' Southeast," Jack said.

"Impossible," Bogie said.

"Hair from a wig rules out the potential for any DNA matching, huh?" Jack asked.

"Well, no, it's a human hair, albeit a dead human hair. Chances are the DNA is from someone who donated or sold that hair for the express purpose of making a wig," Bogie said. "So, I doubt if we'd get any kind of match using that."

"Shit," Jack snarled.

"My sentiments exactly," Bogie said. "But, good news is we now have one solid piece of evidence. Maybe she's getting careless, maybe she's actually trying to leave us clues, you know."

"I somehow get the feeling this person knows exactly what's going on with us," Jackson said, his voice low, "and as you have just pointed out, Bogie, that clue she left us, if it is a she, is actually of no use to us."

"Damn, Jackson, you are one depressing ass," Marvin said, stomping off, "can't let us feel good about something, got to shoot it down every time."

"Just stating facts, buddy," Jack said, going toward his desk.

CHAPTER 14

The first chance Jack got to break away from the investigation into the second homicide, he headed to Gillian's, was grateful when she answered the door, seeing her face register pleasure that he was there. She stepped into his arms, hugging her body to his, turning her face up for a kiss. Without saying a word, he took her to the bedroom, made love to her, furtively, desperately; trying to will the images away, forget everything but his body, hers. Unlike his ex-wife, Gillian seemed to understand these feelings in him, her body responding to his, never questioning his need for physical action without words, somehow being simultaneously submissive yet assertive.

Afterward, they lay entwined together, breathing heavily, the sheet and comforter atangle at the bottom of the bed. Gillian raised up, looked into his eyes, and seeming to understand his desperation, whispered, "Turn over on your stomach. I'll help you relax."

He mutely did as she requested, felt her straddle him, her still-moist warmth as she sat on his lower back, moaned audibly when she placed her warm fingers on his back, began kneading, working magic.

He felt his body begin to react to her probing fingers, the sweet heaviness as he began to relax.

"It happened again," she said, her voice low, making more a statement than question. He felt her lift off him as she shifted, then heard her open the nightstand drawer, pull something out, then close it, her weight settling back onto him again.

He sighed, thinking again of the murder scene.

"Would it help to talk about it?" she asked, her hands placing oil on his skin, moving to his mid back.

"You know I'm not supposed to discuss these things, Gil," he murmured.

"Yeah, but wouldn't this come under the term pillow talk?" she teased.

He grinned into the sheet.

"Come on, Jack. I'm a court reporter. I'm sworn to confidentiality

WAYNE'S DEAD

every time I sit down at my machine. You know you can trust me."
"It's not that, babe, it's just, I don't want to think about it."
"I think you can't help but think about it," she murmured, kissing the nape of his neck.
He sighed again. "If only we could get a handle on this," he said with frustration.
"What have you got so far?" she asked, her voice benign, still kneading.
"Not much. No evidence of any kind to speak of. The only thing of substance, and this is probably a coincidence, is a black-headed woman in a trench coat on the security videos at each hotel the night of the murders."
"A black-headed woman?"
"Yeah."
Gillian was silent a moment "You think the killer's a woman?" she asked.
Jack noticed her voice had changed, was harder than normal. He raised up slightly and looked over his shoulder at her. Her eyes were darker, appearing almost cold. He turned over on his back, placing his hands on Gillian's waist, keeping her astraddle.
"Bogie and Marvin are thinking along those lines, but I gotta say, I'm not sure I agree." He rubbed his hands over his face. "These are vicious, violent murders, Gil, it's hard for me to believe a woman could do that."
"You're such a romantic, Jack," she said, grinning at him.
He looked at her.
"You have this idealized way of looking at women, you know," she said. "Like we're all fragile little things in need of protection."
He gave her a teasing smile. "Well, aren't you?"
She leaned down into his face. "You make me feel secure, Jackson," she whispered, kissing him. "You make me feel safe."
He kissed back, his hands moving over her body. After awhile, she stopped kissing him, sat up. "Hey, what if that woman you're seeing in the videos isn't actually a woman but a man dressed as a woman?"
Jack nodded his head. "I've thought about that, you know, that our killer may be a transvestite. Stats seem to show most murders involving dismemberment or mutilation are committed by

homosexuals."

"I think I read that somewhere," she said. "What do Bogie and Marvin think?"

"Bogie's strong in his belief it's a woman, and I got to tell you, Gil, that guy's good. It's like he almost has a psychic sense about these things."

"Maybe you ought to consider what he says," Gillian replied, watching him.

"Oh, baby, I always take what Bogie says to heart. He's not one you wouldn't want to consider."

She nodded her head.

"Each of the men has been heterosexual, as far as we can determine, so it's only logical we're dealing with a transvestite," Jack went on. "A woman, allegedly, could lure the victim to a hotel room more easily than a man." He shook his head. "It's just hard for me to picture a woman so cold, so heartless to kill a man, then mutilate him, to literally use a body part as a writing instrument and his blood as ink."

"You mean, each one of these men has been dismembered in some way?" she asked, her eyes wide.

"Yeah. Both victims have had their left nut cut off."

She was quiet a moment, then said, "My father didn't have a left testicle," her voice small.

He looked at her. "Really?"

"Yes. He had some sort of infection, supposedly, and had to have it removed, when I was fairly small. You would think losing it would have toned him down, you know. Kind of like neutering a cat or a dog. Not my dad. Talk about a lecherous old fart. He couldn't leave me alone, not even after . . ."

"He wouldn't leave you alone?" Jack asked, stiffening, sitting up, looking into her face.

She shrugged her shoulders, said, "Well, females. I was speaking generally, you know." She pushed him back down onto the bed.

He looked her in the eye. "Did he hurt you, Gil?" he asked, his voice concerned.

She looked away. "He did things," she said, her voice small. "When I was little. That's why I – " She gave him a helpless look, then shrugged. Her lips seemed to quiver as she formed them into a smile. "It's all in the past anyway," she said, her voice sounding almost shrill. She turned her head away. "I don't want to talk about it, it happened years ago. Besides, he's dead now, so what does it matter?"

She seemed to remember Jack then, gave him a quick smile, leaned away from him, pulled open the nightstand drawer. When she looked back at him, she had a mischievous look in her eyes, leaned toward him, whispered, "Do me a favor?"

"Sure."

"Turn over, lie there very quietly and close your eyes and just feel what I'm doing to your body."

"Gil."

"Hush, Jackson. This is my bed and my house and I am determined you will leave here feeling much better. Now, do as I say, and I promise, you won't regret it." Again that impish grin.

He couldn't help but smile back, turned over, lay down, closed his eyes, sighed as she massaged the warm oil onto his lower back and buttocks, then between, heard the soft purring whine of a small motor, felt the vibration as she placed it on his skin, moving it over his back, stiffened slightly as he felt her move it around the anal cleft, then between, then gently, barely inserting it, probing slightly, opened his mouth to protest, but by then the pleasure was too intense, so instead, loudly moaned. Her other hand nudged him onto his side, then came toward his front, found him, followed quickly by her mouth.

Afterward, he insisted she let him give her a body massage, thankful to have found a woman who seemed to know how to relax him so poignantly. He positioned her over a pillow, noticed a bruise on her left hip, reached out, traced it. She glanced back at him.

"That's an awful nasty bruise," he said, looking at her.

Gillian studied it quietly, then said, "I'm such a klutz, I must have run into something and didn't even know it."

"You didn't feel it when you got it?" Jack asked, tracing the ugly purplish-yellowish-greenish colors.

She shrugged. "I'm so fair, Jack, I bruise at the slightest touch."

He leaned down, kissed the area, causing her to giggle, then reached for the bottle of body oil on the nightstand, but it was almost empty. "You got anymore of this stuff, Gil?" he asked, holding it over her shoulder so she could see.

"No, but there's baby oil in the bathroom," she said, "in the vanity, bottom left-hand side."

He got up and ambled into the bathroom. "Damn, I feel good," he said out loud, hearing her laugh behind him.

He rummaged around in the bottom of the vanity but didn't see any. "I can't find it," he called out.

"It's got to be in there, I just used it this morning," Gillian replied, sounding sleepy.

Jack opened up the middle section and began shifting items, came upon a package of condoms, the female variety. He studied the box, looking at them, then glanced into the bedroom. He opened up the package, looked at the condom, then went to the door going into the bedroom.

"Hey, Gil?" he said.

"Hmm?" she answered drowsily.

"You use these things?" he asked, holding it up.

Gillian raised up, looked at it, seeming almost confused by it. Then, "Oh, gosh, no, not for a long time. I didn't even know I had those things," she finally said. "Besides, Jack, I've got you now, I don't need to worry about anything like that anymore, do I?"

"I've never actually seen one," he said, studying it once more.

"They're not a real popular item, in fact, I don't even know if they even make them anymore," Gil said, then, "Did you find the baby oil, darlin', I'm getting impatient."

He grinned at her, went back into the bathroom, put the package back where he found it, opened the right-handed side, found the baby oil, said, "Ah ha," as he went back into the bedroom.

"It's about time," she teased. "I was getting ready to start without you."

The next morning, Jack called his ex-wife, asked if he could see her alone for a few minutes whenever she had some free time. Seeming to misunderstand why, she said she would come to his apartment that night.

"Uh, Bethany, I just need to talk to you, ask you about something I need some information on, within your field. Why don't we meet somewhere for coffee, it'll only take a few minutes, I promise."

They met at the coffee shop they used to frequent when they were married. Bethany was already seated at a booth and smiled wryly when she saw him, offered her cheek for a kiss, then waited for him to sit across from her.

"Well, what's so important we have to talk in private?" she asked, raising one eyebrow, glancing around, as if to say, this isn't the most private place in the world.

"Just wanted to pick your brain a little," Jack said, giving her a tight smile.

"Ah," she said, smiling wider now.

"Ah," he answered sarcastically.

The waitress came and they ordered their drinks. After she left, Bethany settled back, eyeing Jack a little suspiciously.

"You look great," he offered.

She nodded her head as if agreeing.

He cleared his throat.

She waited.

Finally giving in to impatience, she leaned toward him, said, "Well, come on, Jack, ask me whatever it is you're wanting to so I can get out of here. I don't have all day, you know." She was irritated he hadn't wanted to see her at his apartment that evening. She hadn't heard from him in awhile and had been thinking a tryst under the covers with Jack was just the kind of release she needed, but his disinterest was disconcerting to her. Jack had always been easy in that department.

Jack looked away, then back. Leaned toward her, hesitated, leaned back, then toward her again.

"I was just wondering," he began.

"Wondering," she said, nodding her head.

"Bethany, don't make this harder on me than it already is," he snapped at her.

She sighed. "Okay, Jack, I'll just sit here and wait for you to tell me, whenever the hell you think that might be."

His lips tightened. She knew he was getting angry. He seemed to force himself to calm down, then leaned toward her again. "This, I assume, is part of your field of expertise," he said.

Bethany made herself stay silent, cutting off the snipping remark she had to that one.

Jack looked away again, then back. He seemed embarrassed. "When a woman can't, say, achieve climax, even though she seems to want to very much, and even though she's not frigid, you know, she's very warm and loving and responsive, very passionate, what would possibly cause her to be unable to finish?" he asked in a rush, then leaned back, as if relieved.

The new girlfriend, Bethany thought, growing jealous.

"I was just wondering," he said, misreading her look, "if the cause could be from something that happened to her as a child or possibly medical or what," finishing lamely.

Bethany smiled with her mouth. Her eyes were hard, black coals. "Are you asking this for a professional or personal reason?" she asked, making her voice light.

"Does it matter?"

She sighed again. "Okay, we won't go there."

"Let's not."

"Well, Jack, there are several reasons a woman may be unable to achieve an orgasm," she finally said.

He nodded his head.

"Psychological as well as physiological. The first thing she should do is to go to her gynecologist and have an examination, to rule out anything that could be interfering with that, let's call it, goal. If everything checks out there, then it could be more to do with the mind than the body."

"Such as?" he asked, looking interested.

She hesitated, watching him. *God, he must really love her*, she thought to herself, feeling hurt, then sighed again, trying to control her emotions. "Well, okay, she could have been abused, sexually or physically, as a child, and we all know the scars that can leave a young girl with."

Jack nodded his head.

"Or maybe both her parents, or mother or father, either one, taught her while she was growing up that sex is bad, sex is nasty, sex is not something to be enjoyed. That could interfere. Or she could possibly have been raped at as a teenager or adult. That certainly would present problems."

Jack studied his knuckles, nodding his head, then, "Well, what can be done for that?" he finally asked.

"Therapy, of course," she snapped, then unable to hold it back any longer, "This is someone you're involved with, isn't it?"

He frowned at her. "That's really none of your business, Bethany."

"Who are you seeing, Jack? How long has this been going on? Were you fucking her when you were fucking me?" she asked, her face reddening.

"I'm not going to answer that," he said, his voice low, brittle.

"That's how she got the hook in so deep, isn't it?" Bethany hissed.

He looked up, confused. "What?" he asked, frowning at her.

"Oh, come on, Jack, you and I both know you're always going around trying to fix things you feel are broken, trying to fit all the little pieces back together. Always trying to protect those who can't fend for themselves. That's why you're a detective, in case you hadn't figured that out by now, that's why you're a cop. And now, look, along comes this little bitch who just so happens to be frigid and there's big, bad Jackson Daniels more than willing to help her with that particular problem!"

"Shut up," he said, his voice low.

"I'll give it to her, she's more perceptive than I am," Bethany went on, ignoring him. "I mean it took me, what, a year, maybe two before I caught on to that aspect of your character. Which, by the way, I find to be a major personality flaw."

He stood.

"Maybe I should have used that ruse on you, Jack, what do you think? Oh, Jack, honey, I try so hard, but I just can't come when you make love to me. Whatever could be wrong with me? Can you help me?" she asked, her voice mocking.

"You're not only a bitch, but you're a mean, cruel bitch," he said, his voice low. "I regret having even known you."

Bethany felt like she'd been slapped.

Jack turned around and walked out.

Bethany glanced around, wondering if anyone had heard his last remark, then fished through her purse, threw some ones down on the table, got up and left, her face red.

CHAPTER 15

She sits in the chair in front of the psychologist's desk, her legs crossed, watching him react to her confessions. She senses a fear in this man now, wonders if she will have to kill him. Thinks she probably will. Squirms with delight at the fact.

She finally decides to speak. "I don't feel as if you are helping me, Dr. Barnard," she says, her voice husky.

"This takes time," he says, running a shaky hand over his face.

"You seem nervous," she observes.

He looks at her with alarm.

She smiles knowingly.

"You've given me quite a lot to think about," he says, waving his hand at his notes.

"In case you haven't caught on, the killings are symbolic," Ronnie says, watching him closely.

He nods, his face pale as watered milk, fighting the urge to bolt.

"You're not thinking of doing anything about what I've told you?" she asks, her voice hard.

"No, of course not. As I told you at the beginning, you're protected by doctor-patient confidentiality. I can't repeat what you've told me." He desperately tries to remember what exactly the doctor-patient confidentiality entails, wonders if he can legally go to the police without direct knowledge that she will kill again. Decides to seek the services of an attorney after she has left. That is, if he is still alive.

She settles back. "As they're dying," she continues, interrupting his thoughts, "I look into their eyes. It's very interesting, what you see." She stares at him with interest. "Have you ever watched anyone die, Dr. Barnard?" she asks, smiling winningly.

"Uh, no, I'm afraid not," he says, sweat breaking on his face.

"Oh, such a shame," she murmurs. "Perhaps I'll let you watch one day. Would you like that?"

He frowns, then says, "No, I don't think so."

She shrugs nonchalantly. "Your choice, Doctor."

He fidgets, playing with a paper clip on his desk, finally looking back at her. She smiles knowingly. He is sure she senses his fear of her. He hates her, wishes he had never agreed to see her.

"Ronnie, I'm afraid I'm going to have to terminate treatment," he finally says.

"You can't do that!" she screams at him, startling him.

"As long as you're committing these crimes, I'm afraid I can't help you," he quickly adds. "I couldn't in good conscience continue to treat someone I knew was committing such atrocious acts. I think perhaps you should seek the services of a lawyer, turn yourself into the police, admit what you've done. I would be willing to assist if you should seek to defend yourself in the psychological sense. I'm sure you could work something out."

She stares at him, her eyes icy cold, then says, her voice lower, spiteful, "That is out of the question, Doctor. And I would suggest you think of what the future might hold for you if you terminate services."

He is blatantly aware of the threat she is issuing and sits there, thinking, trying to find some way to buy time for himself, already weighing the consequences of going to another area, starting over. He finally says, "All right, if you would be willing to contract with me that as long as I am seeing you, providing treatment to you, you will cease with these killings you've been telling me about, I will agree to continue on. Otherwise, I'm afraid I have no choice but to terminate."

She ponders this for a moment, then smiles engagingly, "Of course," she answers.

"You're willing to contract to that?"

"If you think it's appropriate, I'll do it," she says.

"You will not commit anymore murders?" he asks, suspicious.

"Not as long as you're treating me, Doctor." She holds up her right hand and states, solemnly, "Swear to God." She rises to leave, then adds, "Besides, maybe I'm just delusional, Doctor. Maybe the crimes I've told you about haven't actually occurred. Think about that," and is gone.

93

CHAPTER 16

He was riding her, working, working, moving rhythmically, his body covered with sweat, holding back, watching, waiting. She was close to release, he knew it, closer than she had ever been. She felt like liquid fire inside. Her body was heavy, her forehead and upper lip beaded with sweat. Her eyes were closed, her back and neck arched slightly. She was making low moaning sounds in the back of her throat with each thrust.

The phone began to ring, but he barely registered it at first, not till she started to move restlessly, opening her eyes, stiffening somewhat. The phone stopped. He leaned down, put his mouth on hers, kissed her deeply, willing her to the place she had been before. The ringing started again. She sighed, opened her eyes, said, "I better get that," sounding out of breath.

"Damn!" Jack growled, frustrated.

"I'm sorry," she said, her voice small.

"I'm not mad at you, Gil," he replied, his voice gentle.

She reached out, picked up the receiver, said, "Hello," breathless.

She listened, then held the phone out to him. He gave her a questioning look, then took it. "Daniels," he mouthed into the phone in a gravelly voice.

"You best be getting off your girlfriend and getting on over here," Marvin said, sounding amused.

"Shit fire!"

"You ain't gonna think that when I tell you what's going on," Marvin observed.

Jack rolled off Gillian onto his back, saying, "What?" rubbing his forehead.

"We got us another killing," Marvin said in a solemn voice.

Jack sat up. "When?"

"Last night looks like, although it ain't in our jurisdiction, bro. We're damn lucky one of the detectives in their department gets the Knoxville paper."

"Where?"

"Hotel in Gatlinburg, Tennessee, but there's a problem."

94

"Ain't there always?" Jack asked, his voice acerbic.

"The body was found around nine o'clock. Maid went in to turn the bed down and surprise, surprise."

"Male, I suppose," Jack said.

"Yep."

"So, what's the problem?"

"Crime scene has been investigated and released."

Jack groaned. "Jesus," he said, then, "I thought you said one of the detectives – "

"Yeah, but that was this morning. He wasn't one of the dicks investigating the homicide last night."

Jack glanced over at Gillian, who was lying on her back, watching him. He smiled at her, put his hand out, gently rubbed the side of her face with the backs of his index and middle fingers.

"Bogie's up there now, he left about half an hour ago, soon as we heard. Which is about how long I've been trying to locate you. You care to tell me where the hell your beeper is?" Marvin asked, his voice rising angrily.

Jack looked at the nightstand. "Ah, damn, it's on vibrate. I guess I forgot to change it over before I took it off."

"You know your girlfriend's number's unlisted, man? You know that. I know you know that, but you, for some reason I cannot understand, have not supplied that number to us. You know what I had to do? Had to call her business number, got her frigging answering service, had to practically threaten to come over there and close that place down before they'd give me the damn number. Hope you're happy you put me through all this shit when we could have been – "

"I'm on my way," Jack said, hanging the phone up.

He turned to Gillian. "I'm sorry, babe, but I've got to go."

"Another one?" she asked, sitting up.

He nodded, getting up, reaching for his pants. She watched him as he hurriedly dressed, then came to her. "Sorry about the interruption," he said, leaning down to kiss her.

"Jack, about last night, I'm really sorry I forgot we were supposed to – " she started.

"Let's not talk about that now," he said, feeling himself tense up, remembering.

95

She smiled languidly at him. "I was having a very good time," she said. "I hope when you're through, you'll come back and finish what you started."

"Why don't you hang out at my apartment, wait on me there, I'll see what I can do when I get done," he said, kissing her harder.

"I'm all tingly with anticipation," she teased, smiling.

Marvin was waiting at the station and didn't say anything when Jack pulled up, just got in, slammed the door hard, signaling his irritation.

Jack sighed. "Listen, I'm sorry, okay?" he said. "I didn't think, all right?"

Marvin folded his arms, glaring out the windshield.

Jack huffed. He knew he was going to have to hand over something personal to Marvin to distract him or else he'd have to put up with his pissy mood all day long. "Listen, guy, Gil and I had a date last night, but she got tied up and didn't make it, and when she called me this morning, I – well you know how it is, I was anxious to see her."

Jack stopped, glanced at Marvin, saw it was going to take more. "Shit, Marvin, she's got me so tied up in knots it ain't even funny," he said, pulling out a cigarette, placing it in his mouth.

"What have I told you about smoking in the car?" Marvin asked, sounding like a nagging wife.

Jack looked at him. "I'll roll down the window," he said.

"Nuh-uh," Marvin answered. "We have discussed this very subject before, and you will recall that we agreed, while we are confined in a car together, you will not smoke. You want to kill yourself, you go right on ahead, but you ain't taking me along with you, hurrying my death up, nun-uh, no way. You know how dangerous second-hand smoke is. I showed you the statistics."

Jack flipped the cigarette into the back seat.

"Oh, so, now the man's gonna pout," Marvin said, seeing Jack's face, nodding his head. "Got interrupted in his lovemaking, can't smoke his cigarette, gonna have himself a major pout."

Jack glared at him.

"So, you want to expound on this theory you were espousing?" Marvin asked.

Jack ignored him.

"About your woman," Marvin encouraged.

"I don't think so," Jack said.

"She got you tied up in knots, huh?" Marvin asked. He studied Jack a moment, then said, "Well, that sure ain't the Jackson Daniels I've known all these years, that cold-hearted mother couldn't stand the thought of getting close to a woman, not even his own wife."

Jack studied the road.

After a few minutes of silence, Marvin said, "What'd she do, stand you up last night?" Seeing Jack stiffen at this, he nodded his head. "She playing games with your head, man, fucking with your mind as well as your body?"

"I don't know, man," Jack said, reaching for another cigarette, then stopping. "It's like she forgets, you know, gets involved in whatever she's doing and doesn't remember we have plans."

"You said anything to her about that?"

"Yeah, I tried talking to her about it. She knows it pisses me off, but every time, she's got some sort of excuse, and before I know it, she's got me in the bedroom, apologizing, feeling contrite, wanting to make it up to me, and, well, you know."

"Don't take you long to forget what you were mad about to start with," Marvin finished.

Jack didn't answer.

"You reckon she's doing it on purpose or just forgets like she says? Some people are like that, you know," Marvin said.

Jack glanced at him. "No, I don't think she's playing games," he said, then sighed.

"What?" Marvin asked.

"I don't know, it makes me feel like maybe I care more for her, about being with her, than she does me. At least until I see her and she convinces me otherwise."

Marvin nodded his head. "I dated a girl like that once, man, she had me going in circles."

"Yeah?"

"It was like if I couldn't see her when I wanted to see her, that made me want to see her more, and by the time I did see her, I was like a bull, ranting and raving, then rutting away like no tomorrow."

Jack laughed.

"I reckon you're feeling the same way," Marvin observed.

Jack stayed silent.

"So it's that serious, huh?" Marvin asked, pushing.

When Jack didn't answer, he said, "You're moving pretty quick, there, partner, maybe you ought to back off a little, slow down."

Jack gave him a look, then said, "Marvin, my man, if I could, I would."

Marvin nodded his head understandingly.

When they got to the hotel, Jack was back in a foul mood, feeling guilty about leaving Gillian so hurriedly, not even being able to talk to her about what had been going on with her body before the damn frigging phone rang, then growing angry with her that she had stood him up once more, even angrier with himself that he had forgiven her so easily. He got out of the car, practically ran into the hotel and to the elevator, counting on Marvin to know the room number.

Bogie was inside, alone, studying pictures, looking at the room, doing his own drawings, making notes. Jack glanced at the wall over the headboard. Same message, although smeared. "Like that?" he asked, pointing to the bloody rivulets, now pink in color.

Bogie, getting his meaning, shook his head no. "The hotel had a cleanup crew in here, they were scrubbing it down, till I made them stop."

"They disturb very much?" Jack asked.

"Nah, we've got the pictures, the techs have the evidence."

Jack and Marvin stopped touring the room, looked at him. "Of which so far there is no clue as to who our killer actually is," Bogie said, answering them.

Jack shook his head disgustedly, then went over to Bogie, took the pictures from him, began leafing through them.

"Where'd you get these?" Jack asked.

"Stopped by the sheriff's office, they had them waiting on me, along with some preliminary reports," Bogie answered, then recited, "White male, approximately 45 to 50 years of age," his voice clinical. "As with the others, sans left testicle, which was used as the writing instrument, then discarded on the floor. He died after ejaculation per a condom found on the deceased's penis. No distinguishable prints on the drinking glasses other than the victim's. Nothing in the bathroom. Same round hole in the thorax region, over the heart. Cause of death is exactly the same as the others."

They looked at each other.

"Damn, this killer's good," Marvin said.

"Anybody ID the body yet?" Jack asked.

Bogie glanced at him. "I don't know. The detectives who caught the call are supposed to be on their way over so we can compare notes. Maybe they'll have something."

Jack looked through the pictures again. "What's this around his wrists?" he asked Bogie, handing over one of the photos.

Bogie studied it, then said, "Looks like a contusion of some sort, maybe a ligature."

The door to the suite opened and two tall, heavy-set men strode into the room. They were dressed entirely in black and appeared almost identical except one had blond hair, the other brown.

They introduced themselves as Detectives Rinaka and Weimer. *Weird guys to go with weird names,* thought Jack.

Jack and Marvin listened as Bogie queried the detectives on what exactly they had found.

"Exactly what's depicted in the pictures," Rinaka said, pointing.

"Nothing was moved, changed beforehand?" Bogie asked.

"Nah, we know better than that," Weimer said, acting irritated. "We let the techs do their work before we even attempted to investigate."

Bogie nodded his head.

"What about those marks around his wrists?" Jack asked, pulling the photograph out, handing it over.

The two men smiled. "Handcuffs," they said, in unison.

"He was handcuffed?" Marvin asked.

They grinned in unison.

"When you found him?" Bogie asked.

"No, man, we found them in the bathroom. Must have been into kinky sex, what do you think?"

"You find anything else in the bathroom?" Bogie asked.

"Just the handcuffs," Rinaka answered.

"Fingerprints?" Marvin asked.

"Shit no. This whole place was clean. Only distinguishable prints to be found belonged to the victim."

"You ID'd him yet?" Jack asked.

They smiled again.

"Must have been an attorney-at-law," Marvin said, seeing their grins.

"Yeah, a real prominent divorce attorney. Pretty well known all over east Tennessee," Weimer answered.

"Yeah?" Jack looked at the photographs again. "I don't recognize him," he said.

"Might be 'cause he's missing his hairpiece." Rinaka said, smirking.

Jack looked at the pictures again. "Shit, is that Locker Johnson?" he asked, looking closer.

The two detectives laughed in answer.

"You knew him?" Marvin asked.

"What do you think? That scuzz was Bethany's divorce attorney," Jack said, throwing the pictures on the table.

"He live here?" Bogie asked.

"Nah, lives in Knoxville," Rinaka said.

"He married?" Marvin asked.

"Going through a divorce," Weimer said.

Jack, Bogie, and Marvin looked at the other two detectives.

"We checked on the soon-to-be ex," Rinaka answered their unspoken question. "She's out of the country."

"That's been an awful convenient alibi in the past," Marvin said.

"Yeah, but from what we've been told, they were still pretty friendly with each other," Rinaka said.

"Amicable divorce, they call it," Weimer added.

"Did you check for a security tape at the front desk?" Jack asked.

Rinaka nodded. "Yeah, we viewed most of it last night, finished up this morning."

"You happen to notice a black-headed woman wearing a trench coat and sunglasses amble by?" Marvin asked.

The two detectives looked at each other, thinking.

"Anybody wearing sunglasses would have caught our attention right off," Weimer said. "We didn't notice anybody like that."

"What about a dark-headed woman wearing a trench coat, sans sunglasses?" Bogie asked.

They paused, thinking, then both shook their head no. "It was warm last night, the trench coat would have stuck out, too," Rinaka said.

"The dude sign in as John Wayne?" Marvin asked.

"Yep, the Duke himself," Weimer said. He looked at the others. "Your victims sign in the same way?"

Jack nodded. "You matched the victim's handwriting yet to the registration card?"

"Yeah," Rinaka said. "We met his secretary early this morning, she confirmed that was her boss's handwriting on the registration card."

"I take it there were no witnesses to be found," Bogie said drily.

Weimer and Rinaka shook their heads sadly.

"You checked out the last people to see this dude alive?" Marvin asked.

"We been working on that this morning," Weimer said. "His secretary said he left early yesterday, told her he was going to take the day off, go home, work on a book he was writing."

They stood around looking at each other.

"Are we gonna have a problem with anyone getting territorial here?" Jack finally asked.

Rinaka and Weimer looked at each other, then at Jack. "Long as you share with us, we'll share with you," Weimer said, Rinaka nodding assent.

"Okay, sounds good to me," Jack replied, glancing around the room again. "Those pictures for our use?" he asked them.

They nodded in unison.

He looked at Bogie. "You got anything you need to do, Bogie? Anything you want to check?"

Bogie shook his head, walking around the room, seeming to be sniffing the air.

"He all right?" Rinaka asked.

"Yeah, man, he's just fine," Marvin said. "Got the nose of a bloodhound. You smell anything, Boge?"

Bogie glanced at them, then walked into the bathroom. When he came out, he looked happy. "Same cinnamony smell as the others," he said. "It's got to be perfume."

"Or aftershave," Jack put in.

"Could be a scented candle," Marvin added.

"You guys thinking a woman is doing this shit?" Rinaka asked, looking amused.

Bogie and Marvin nodded their heads.

"We're not sure," Jack answered. "We're considering all possibilities at this point."

"Damnation," Weimer and Rinaka said in unison, sounding respectful.

After they shook hands all around and agreed once more to share any new material that developed, Jack, Marvin and Bogie left, walking to the elevator together.

"Well, ain't no doubt this is our killer," Jack said.

"Think it could have been a client, maybe at one point or another used each of these guys?" Marvin asked as they stepped onto the elevator.

Bogie pondered. "I think it's someone who has access to attorneys, has a way of meeting them, knowing them."

"You mean like a judge, somebody like that?" Marvin asked.

Bogie nodded. "Court clerk, paralegal, secretary, anybody," he said.

"Or court reporter," Jack said. "That's what Gillian does and she's around attorneys all the time."

Marvin shook his head in frustration. "It'd take an army just to begin to investigate all the people who come into contact with attorneys," he said.

When they got to the lobby, Jack stopped Bogie by putting his hand on his arm. "I've been thinking about those condoms," he said, "the fact that no secretions are on the outside of them, nothing."

"Yeah?"

"Okay, I know this could possibly advance your theory, Boge, but what if the perp is wearing one of those female condoms, you know, the ones that are inserted vaginally?"

There was a pause as Bogie thought this over. "Damn, Jack, I don't know why I didn't think of that," he finally said.

"Shit, man, that's good thinking on your part," Marvin said, his tone respectful.

Jack didn't bother telling them what had brought about his realization.

"It could be a man, you know, inserts one into his anus before intercourse," Jack offered.

"Back to the transvestite theory, huh?" Marvin asked.

Jack sighed. "I just can't visualize a woman having that kind of rage, mutilating a man like that."

Bogie chuckled. "You were definitely born in the wrong century, son."

Marvin looked at him. "Let me ask you something, Jack. You were married for how long, five years, to one of the coldest bitches I have ever known. You telling me you can't see her getting mad at someone, say you, going after you with a knife or whatever, killing you, then mutilating you after the fact? You telling me you can't see Bethany doing that to nobody?"

Jack thought. "Actually, no. Okay, she's got a temper, she gets mad, she gets physical. That's one of the reasons I divorced her, but I can't see her mutilating a man like that."

Marvin shook his head, giving Jack a sad look. "Partner, I got to tell you, you are not in this time zone. Women today are just as mean and violent as the men are, don't you see? It's that equality thing they're spouting off about. You've seen it before, you know how mean and bloody they can get. How long you been a detective? What about that woman that cut up her husband in little, bitty pieces and left him scattered all over Knoxville last year? Took Bogie around, showing him where all the parts were? You remember that?"

"Of course I do, Marvin, but you forget, she didn't actually do the cutting, her boyfriend did."

"Oh, well, yeah, but she directed him to, she watched. You telling me she wouldn't have done it if he hadn't had? Nah, I don't think so."

Jack sighed. "Okay, I concede, it's probably a woman, but damn, it's got to be some pretty powerful woman to inflict that kind of harm on a man."

"Or a pretty rageful one," Bogie said.

Jack looked at him, nodding his head.

It was late evening when Jack got home. When he opened the door to his apartment, he was disappointed to see no lights on, indicating to him Gillian wasn't there. He had hoped she would wait there like she promised.

Not bothering with the lights, he went into the kitchen, put his keys down on the counter, unstrapped his shoulder holster, put it and his gun on top of the refrigerator, then opened it, took out a quart of orange juice, stood there drinking from the carton, putting it back when he was finished.

He closed the door and immediately felt hackles rise on the back of his neck. He turned around quickly but could ascertain nothing out of the ordinary in the dark.

He put his agitation down to nerves. *Who wouldn't have a case of the jitters*, he thought to himself, *after what I've seen lately*, as he stepped into the hall, then went into the extra bedroom he used for an office. He turned on the small desk lamp, gathered up files he had placed in there, intending to take them to bed with him so he could go over them before going to sleep. He never slept for hours after investigating a homicide and thought he could put the time to better use than lying in bed staring at the ceiling.

He turned off the desk lamp, stepped into the hallway and stopped, feeling goose bumps come up on his arms, feeling a presence with him. He reached out quickly, flipped on the light switch. He turned and looked behind him, then forward. Not seeing anything, he went closer to his bedroom. The door was shut, which was out of the ordinary; he always kept it open. He began feeling hopeful maybe Gillian was there, in bed, and opened the door, looking in that direction.

He felt movement to his left and turned quickly. Gillian was there, her arms raised over her head, the light from the hallway catching a silvery glint protruding from her hands.

"Gil?" he asked, startled, stepping back out of harm's way. She seemed to jolt, then he heard her gasp.

"Shit, Gil, what the hell are you doing?" he asked, feeling along the wall, finding the light switch, turning it on, his eyes widening when he saw the butcher knife.

Gillian's eyes followed his, seeming to startle at the sight of the knife in her hands as if she didn't know it was there, then dropped it as if it were something repulsive, her hands flying to her mouth.

"Oh, God, Jack, I'm so sorry, I don't know what I was doing," she said, going to him, stepping into his arms.

"Honey, what the hell were you doing with a knife?" he asked her.

She was trembling. He pulled her away, looking into her face. "I–

I guess I was scared," she said. "I heard someone in the apartment, and it was so dark, and I figured if it was you, you'd turn the lights on, so I guess I thought it must be a prowler, a burglar, I don't know, someone other than you. So, I must have got a knife and, oh, God, Jack, if I'd have hurt you I couldn't live with myself," she said, bursting into tears.

"It's okay, babe," he said, hugging her to him, wondering vaguely about what she had just said that didn't sound quite right to him. "You were scared. It's all right. I should have turned the lights on. I didn't think you were here, so I was just going to go onto bed."

She clung to him. "You mean so much to me," she mumbled into his shoulder. "You mean the world to me, Jack. No one's ever meant as much to me as you do. I couldn't stand it if anything happened to you." She pulled back, began kissing him passionately, furtively.

"Take me to bed," she whispered in his ear. "Make love to me, Jack, let me make love to you," tugging at his shirt.

He picked her up in his arms, kissing her, carried her to the bed, forgetting about the knife on the floor.

CHAPTER 17

A few nights later, Jack and Gillian had just returned to his apartment after having dinner and were heading in the direction of the bedroom when his phone began to ring.

Gillian looked at him. "Don't answer it," she said, her voice urgent, her eyes heavy with passion.

He glanced at the phone, then back to her, giving her a please-forgive-me smile.

"Go ahead," she said, reluctantly smiling back.

He picked the phone up, barking "Daniels" into the receiver, but no one was there.

"Must not have been important," he said, going to her, pulling her into his arms, kissing her urgently. She began backing her way to the bedroom while kissing back, her hands going to the waistband of his jeans, tugging him with her.

His beeper went off.

"Damn!" Gillian said, with frustration.

"Sorry, babe," Jack murmured, plucking it off his belt, glancing at the readout.

"It's Marvin," he said, his voice grim.

Gillian made a moaning noise. "Oh, please, not another one," she said, her voice small.

Jack went to the phone by the bed, dialed Marvin's cellular phone number.

His partner answered on the first ring.

"What's up?" Jack asked.

"Man, there is something I need to show you," Marvin said, sounding out of breath.

"Now?" Jack asked with irritation.

"Now," Marvin said, emphatic.

"Is it important?" Jack asked.

"You think I'd be calling you this time of night if it wasn't?" Marvin asked irritably. "Hell, I had plans to spend the evening in bed with my wife, get rid of some of this high testosterone level I got to carry around with me, if you get my drift, so if I'm calling you instead, you know it's important, man."

"Where are you?" Jack asked, glancing at Gillian, who looked disappointed.

"Down in the Old City, place called Farley's," Marvin answered.

"What the hell are you doing in a place like that?" Jack asked.

"Just get here quick, 'cause I don't want to lose this one," Marvin said, then added, "and you know that ornery look you like to wear on your face? Do me a favor and don't come through the door looking like that, 'cause the minute you do you're gonna get pegged as a bull and this place will clear out in ten seconds flat and we're gonna lose what may solve this little killer of a problem we've been having lately, if you know what I'm saying."

"On my way," Jack said, hanging up the phone.

He went to Gillian, kissed her, said, "I gotta go, but maybe this won't take long. Why don't you stay here, wait for me? I'll make it worth your while, I promise."

She smiled at him. "I'll hold you to that promise," she said, unfastening her skirt, wriggling out of it.

He backed out of the room, watching her undress as he went.

Farley's was a nightclub on the outskirts of the Old City, known for its attraction to the gay male population. Jack stepped into the bar, looking around for Marvin, finally catching a glimpse of him at the back of the room.

His partner was sitting at a table alone, drinking a beer, trying to act cool.

"This your kind of place?" Jack said, glancing around, pulling out a seat.

Marvin favored that with a sour expression, causing Jack to grin.

"So, what's going on?" Jack asked, looking around.

Marvin leaned toward him. "Don't look now, I'll tell you when you can, but we got us a transvestite sitting at the bar, looks a lot like the woman we saw on those security tapes."

Jack resisted the impulse to turn his head toward the bar.

A waiter came up, gave Jack a smirk, then asked if he wanted to order anything.

"I'll have what my friend's having," Jack answered, ignoring the knowing nod he received in response from their server.

"You want to tell me anything?" he asked his partner when they were alone.

"Say what?"

"About what you're doing here, dude. We both know what kind of clientele frequents this joint."

Marvin shrugged. "Oh, that. You know my cousin, Vernon, you remember him? Short dude, about as wide as he is tall, kind of stammers when he gets excited?"

Jack thought. "Can't say as I remember Vernon," he said, settling back, smiling.

"Well, Vernon, see, he likes to dress up like a woman from time to time," Marvin explained.

"I see," Jack said, nodding his head, playing with his friend.

"Oh, you thinking I'm the one likes to dress like a woman," Marvin said, catching Jack's look. "You thinking I'm just making this cousin up so you won't think it's me does that sort of thing."

"Hey, man, it's cool, I'm not judgmental," Jack said, holding his palms up. "Whatever turns you on, babe."

Marvin was getting mad. "You want to shut the fuck up and listen to what I'm trying to tell you here?"

Jack sat back, complying.

"Anyway, Vernon, you got to remember him, Jack, he's the one got sent up last year for trying to solicit an undercover cop. I told you about him. Told you about how the family got so riled and all, wanted me to do something about it, thought since I was a cop, I could get it taken care of, like a traffic ticket, remember?"

Jack nodded his head. "Yeah, I remember now. They had you going in circles trying to get old Vern out of trouble."

"Yeah, right, and then he ended up getting put on probation 'cause the sarge knew somebody who knew somebody who owed somebody a favor."

"Saved Vern from becoming some guerilla's boyfriend, I'm sure," Jack said.

Marvin thought, then said, "Maybe we didn't do Vern a favor after all."

Jack and Marvin both laughed at that.

"Okay, look now," Marvin said, "this end of the bar."

Jack turned his head and studied the area, his eyes immediately finding what looked to be a black-headed woman, slenderly built, sitting at the bar, talking to a heavy-set black man beside her.

"That's him?" Jack asked, turning back to Marvin, who nodded affirmation.

"How does Vern come into this?" Jack asked.

"Oh, yeah, well, Vern, he and I was shooting the bull the other day and I remembered how he likes to, you know, from time to time dress up like a woman, go cruising. He says he doesn't do anything, just kind of hangs out, every once in a while. Well, anyway, it ain't really none of my business what he does and I don't care, but I remembered Vern likes to do that, so I told him keep his eyes on the lookout for a man dressed like a woman, you know, fits the description of our alleged killer."

"You didn't tell him it was our killer, did you?" Jack asked.

"Shit no, man, I know better than that. I just told Vernon we were looking for somebody fit that description, may be a witness to a case we were working on, let me know if he ever saw anybody like that."

Jack nodded his head, listening.

"Anyway, Vern, he calls me tonight, you know, right at the most inopportune time, if you get my drift, says he's at Farley's, come on down, he's got something to show me."

"Just like you did me."

"Hey, it's good to know I wasn't the only one had to leave something good," Marvin said.

"Okay, so you came down here," Jack prodded.

"Yeah, and there she, he, whatever, was, sitting at that bar, pretty as you please."

"Does Vernon know this person?" Jack asked.

Marvin glanced at the bar, then back. "Says no, this is the first time he's seen this dude."

"Vernon's here?" Jack asked.

Marvin grimaced. "Yeah, he's at the bar over there near the door, the one with the blond wig and black dress."

Jack turned and looked toward the door, finding a black man with a blond, curly wig, wearing a low-cut black sequined dress. Vernon, catching Jack's eyes, waved. Jack nodded back.

"He looks good for a woman," Jack said to Marvin when he turned back around.

"Yeah, man, I was surprised he looks that good," Marvin said.

"Course, Vernon's always had them pretty features, you know. Only problem is, he's so fat."

"I don't know," Jack said, "from what I hear, there's a lot of men out there like fat women."

"Yeah, Vern says the same thing."

They were silent for a moment.

"Wonder how they get that cleavage look," Jack finally said.

"Wonder how they hide their thing," Marvin shot back.

"You ever asked Vernon?" Jack asked.

"No, man, I figure what he does is – "

"None of your business," Jack finished for him.

"Yeah."

"So, how do you want to handle this, guy?" Jack asked, sitting back, glancing around.

"Well, we got to talk to him, that's for sure," Marvin said.

"Why don't you amble on over there, ask him to come join us?" Jack asked.

"Hey, man, you're the white one sitting at this table, you go ask the dude," Marvin said.

"Way I see it, he's talking to a black guy, so maybe he likes black men," Jack said.

Marvin glared at him.

"Okay, I'll go ask him," Jack said, shoving his chair back, getting up, going toward the bar.

He sidled in next to the dark-headed man dressed like a woman, noticing now the heavy makeup which helped the face to appear more feminine, thinking, damn, if I passed this guy on the street, I'd think he was a woman.

The man turned and looked at him. Jack nodded, the man nodded back.

"My friend and I were just wondering if you'd care to join us at our table," Jack said, nodding his head toward Marvin.

The man studied Marvin, then Jack, then said, "Sure," grabbing his purse and heading in the direction of their table.

Jack followed along behind, amazed that the man could move so well in the spiky heels he wore.

Marvin got up, pulled a chair out for their guest, then sat back down.

Jack sat down next to Marvin, facing the suspect, taking in the silky red dress, made-up face, raven-colored wig, painted and decorated long fingernails. Wondered how he even managed to conceal his Adam's apple, deciding finally this guy had to look more female than male, even without makeup, to be able to carry off this transition so well.

"My name's Jack Daniels," Jack finally said, holding his hand out, shaking, noticing the man's rather small hands, then introduced Marvin.

"Ronald Oberman," the man replied, shaking hands with Marvin, his voice almost too-high for a man, making Jack wonder if he was taking some sort of hormones, going for the sex-change thing in the future. "Although, when I'm dressed like this, I go by Ronnie," Oberman added, giving a slight, trilling laugh. Jack fought the urge to cringe.

Jack pulled his badge out, flipped it open.

"Shit," the man ranted, looking ready to get up and run.

"We just want to ask you some questions," Marvin quickly interjected, "No big deal."

"Am I under arrest?" Ronald asked.

"You done anything wrong?" Jack asked back.

"Listen, dressing up like a woman isn't against the law," Oberman said. "As you can see, I'm not the only one in here doing it, so if you're going to arrest me, you're going to have to arrest every other man in here dressed like a woman."

"We just want to ask you some questions," Marvin repeated, leaning toward Oberman. "You can either sit there and be nice and answer our questions or we can all troop down to the police station and be up half the night playing cat and mouse."

"Do I need an attorney?" Oberman asked.

"Not at this point," Jack said.

Oberman studied them, then said, his voice low. "Listen, I'm a married man. I've got two kids. If my wife knew I was doing this, she'd have my balls. She'd probably take the kids and run, divorce me, take all my money. I don't want that. I don't need that. I only dress this way occasionally. It's no big thing, you know. Just a way to relax, have a different kind of fun."

"Hey, man, it's cool," Marvin said. "We ain't interested in that

111

anyway. Like I told you twice already, we just wanting to ask you some questions."

"About what?" Oberman asked, giving them a suspicious look.

"About where you've been certain nights," Jack said.

Oberman looked at them. "Am I a suspect?" he asked, his eyes widening.

"Not yet," Marvin said. "Keep acting like that and you will be."

Oberman pondered this, then said, "Hey, I got nothing to hide except maybe this from my wife," looking down at his dress. "So, go ahead, ask me anything you want."

Jack nodded, pulled out his notebook. "First off, give me your driver's license," he said.

Oberman opened his purse, pulled it out, gave it to Jack, who jotted down the number, date of birth, and the man's address. "This address current?" he asked.

"Yeah," Oberman answered sullenly.

"Give me your Social Security number," Jack said.

Oberman complied.

"What do you do for a living?" Marvin asked.

"I'm an orthodontist," Oberman said, then gave them his office address and business card.

Jack handed the license back. "Okay, I'm going to write down three dates here, and I want you to tell me where you were and what you were doing on each of those dates, if you can remember."

Oberman looked at Jack, then gave a reluctant nod.

Jack listed the dates of the murders, then handed them to Oberman.

"Just remember, we'll check your alibis," Jack said. "So it would not behoove you to lie about where you were or what you were doing."

"So I am a suspect," Oberman commented.

"You just look like someone we're looking for," Jack replied. "At this point, it goes no further than that."

"Maybe I need to call my lawyer," Oberman said.

"You want to do that, we'll go on down to the station and you can call from there," Marvin stated.

"Dressed like this?" Oberman asked.

"Yep," Marvin said.

Oberman thought about it. "Okay, just give me a second." He studied the list, then said, "Wait a minute," getting into his purse again, pulling out a date book, opening it up.

"Okay, first one on here, back in October, that week my wife and I were on a cruise to the Bahamas, celebrating our tenth wedding anniversary," he said, giving them a grin.

"You got proof?" Jack asked.

"I can get you the canceled tickets. Name of the cruise line was Royal Caribbean. It was one of those week-long cruises. Call the registry and verify I went. I can find my charge card slips where I charged drinks and such on board, paid for scuba diving, where I purchased gifts at Nassau, places like that."

"We need that ASAP," Jack said.

"I'll get it for you tomorrow," Oberman said. "I'll have a courier bring it to you, just tell me where."

"KPD, downtown, tell the courier to bring it personally to me," Jack said.

"You got a card?" Oberman asked.

Jack pulled one out, gave it to him.

Oberman nodded, then went back to the list.

"Okay, this date in December, let's see." He consulted his date book. "That was a Friday night. I was in town. My guess is I spent it with my family." He looked back at Jack. "We usually go out to eat on Friday night. I can't confirm it." He paused. "No, wait a minute, I charge a lot, let me see if I can find a charge receipt for that night."

"What about later that night," Jack asked, "or that afternoon?"

"That afternoon, I was working. Call my office, my office manager will confirm it. That night, of course, I was with my wife." He studied them. "You've got to promise me you won't tell them about why you want the information regarding my whereabouts or finding me like this tonight."

"No problem," Jack said. He smiled. "I'll let you handle that."

Oberman nodded, then went back to the list. "Okay, last month," as he turned pages in his book. He stopped, read, then gave them a smile. "Strike three, you're out," he said. "I was at a dental convention in Atlanta. I can also get you the information verifying that one."

Jack and Marvin looked at each other.

"You sure do a lot of traveling," Marvin said.

Oberman shrugged. "Hey, I make a good living. Why not enjoy it while I can? A convention here, a vacation there, it's all a tax write-off anyway, the way my accountant's got it set up."

Marvin gave Jack a sour look. Jack knew he was thinking the same thing: neither one of them had taken a vacation in years.

Oberman closed his date book. "That it?" he asked.

"You like the Duke?" Marvin segued.

Oberman grinned. "Hey, everybody likes John Wayne," he said, getting up.

"I want that information tomorrow," Jack reminded him.

"No problem," Oberman said.

"Oh, and one other thing, don't go on anymore trips, not until we tell you you can," Marvin said.

"No problem," Oberman repeated, then went back to the bar.

Jack and Marvin sat there thinking. Vernon came over.

"Hey," he said, pulling out a chair and sitting down.

"Hey, man, you dress up good," Jack said, grinning.

"Thanks," Vernon replied, beaming, adjusting his wig.

Marvin pulled out a twenty, handed it to his cousin. "You done good, cuz, thanks," he said.

Vernon leaned toward them. "You want me to keep an eye on this dude for you?" he asked.

Marvin looked at Jack, who shrugged. "Hey, man, that'd be great," Marvin said. "Think you can handle it?"

Vernon puffed up. "No sweat. I'll follow him when he leaves, call you later, let you know where he goes."

Marvin stuck a fist out and he and his cousin went through some procedure Jack never fully understood.

Vernon nodded at Jack, got up, went back to the bar.

"You think Oberman's our guy?" Jack asked Marvin.

Marvin shrugged, then said, "Nah, he seemed too normal, I guess. Not even a little bit off."

"You don't call a man dressing up like a woman and parading around off?" Jack asked with disbelief.

Marvin shrugged. "We can't arrest him, we don't have proof. Hell, don't even have any fingerprints to compare his to even if we wanted."

"Can't even request a surveillance on him," Jack said, watching Vernon watching Oberman.

"Hey, man, if he was guilty, don't you think he would have hightailed it on out of here as soon as we were through talking to him?" Marvin asked.

Jack thought. "Unless he knows that would make him even more suspect. Remember, man, we got us a cold, calculating killer here."

Marvin nodded. "Well, what do you want to do?"

Jack moved restlessly. "You think Vern's reliable?" he asked.

"Hell, man, that dude will do it if it's for me," Marvin answered. "He's cool."

Jack nodded. "Okay, then, why don't I go home to Gillian and you go home to your wife and let's finish what got started?"

Marvin grinned in response.

CHAPTER 18

When Jack walked into the bar and grill frequented by the courthouse crowd, he was mad. He wanted to find some lowlife criminal and pound him into the floor. Do somebody some heavy damage.

He sat down at the bar, ordered a beer, running his hand through his hair, wondering why in hell Gillian couldn't just once be where she was supposed to be.

They had made plans for dinner and he found himself once again stranded outside her apartment, waiting. After an hour, he gave up. Not wanting to go home to an empty abode, he had come here, the local courthouse hangout. He pounded his fist on the bar, mumbled "Sorry" to the bartender who glanced his way, then turned his back, looking toward the door.

"Shit," he muttered to himself. *Why the hell does she keep doing this to me*, he wondered. Never telling him where she had been or what she had been doing, throwing out general excuses, nothing concrete, then always atoning through sex. "Shit," he muttered again, wondering why she did this.

"This has got to stop," he said out loud, then shook his head no to the bartender who headed his way, mistakenly thinking he wanted another round.

An attractive woman wearing a business suit sat down next to him. He glanced her way. "Hi," she said, smiling brightly.

Jack nodded grimly, then turned his back on her.

Marvin came breezing through the door, caught sight of Jack, headed his way.

"Hey, man, what's shaking?" he asked, sitting down, signaling to the bartender.

"Does anybody ever actually say that anymore?" Jack asked the air.

"I just did," Marvin replied affably. He glanced at Jack, then away. "The man's in a dark mood, better watch out," he told the bartender.

Jack frowned.

Marvin ordered a beer, then turned to his partner. "Looks like our transvestite semi checks out," he said.

Jack looked at him.

Marvin nodded. "I spent all afternoon on the phone, checked out all those credit card receipts." He shook his head. "Shit, man, I am in the wrong profession. I am so tired of dealing with people who got money and like to throw it around. They could send some my way if they wanted to, you know." Then seeing Jack's look, continued. "I'll start with the most recent and go backward. He was listed on the roster for the convention in Atlanta, signed in, but hell, Jack, that's only four hours away. He could have driven up here, done the killing, driven back in one evening. We'll have to track down witnesses who can say for sure he was there that particular night at that particular time.

"His wife alibied him for the Friday night of our second killing, his office manager alibied him for that afternoon. 'Course, take that however you want; you know they probably both have an agenda here.

"As far as the cruise, the credit card receipts are all dated and signed, except for one problem, they don't start till the day after the first killing. Oberman told me his wife hates to fly, so they drove down the day of the murder, caught the cruise ship the next day. Wonder why he didn't bother supplying that piece of information when we were talking to him? So, he could have offed the guy, then flown down to Miami, got on the cruise ship, and gone on. But his wife says no, he's telling the truth, they drove down. Still, I've got Robin checking the airline rosters for that night and the day after, heading to Miami." He shrugged. "'Course, he could have driven to Atlanta, caught a plane from there. Hell, man, he could have done just about anything. Anyway, I even went to his office, got his office manager to give me a copy of his signature, had him sign a blank sheet of paper, then checked each one of the signatures on the credit card receipts against his, and they all matched, just in case." Marvin shook his head. "It's starting to look like a lot of paperwork going nowhere so far. Best thing we got is how close he was at the time of our third homicide."

Jack stared grimly ahead.

"So what'd she do this time?" Marvin asked.

Jack shook his head disgustedly.

"Man, you are gonna have to just get over it," Marvin lectured.

Jack glared at him.

"Quit taking everything with that girl so damn personal. Accept her for who she is, what she does. Quit thinking everything she does is to make you mad."

Jack was fuming. "I don't think that," he said, turning to glare.

"Well, you sure act it. Let me guess. She's late again, right? Only doing it on purpose. Only making you wait around for her, getting madder and madder 'cause she, along with the rest of the world, likes to see old Jackson Daniels in one of his bad moods, glaring at everybody, snarling, itching for somebody to take his mood out on."

"Shut up," Jack said, his voice low.

"Maybe she's just one of these people, you know, gets caught up in what they're doing, don't realize where the time goes, what they got planned, you know."

"Yeah?" Jack asked, turning to him.

"Yeah, and you, Jackson, you got to just keep that in mind anytime you plan something with her, you know, she's gonna be late, she ain't gonna be there, whatever, and just go on. Act like it don't bother you, sooner or later, it won't."

"Listen, if we have something planned, I make damn sure I'm where I'm supposed to be, she could at least do the same," Jack snapped at him.

"You told her this?" Marvin asked.

"Yeah, I've told her countless times. All the good it's done me."

"Well, that's just one of her faults, I guess. One of her quirks. Either accept it or reject it, then get over it."

"Marvin, just shut the fuck up," Jack said, throwing down dollar bills on the bar, signaling the bartender. He ran his hands over his face, then glanced at his partner, who was watching him. "Man, I have never let a woman get to me the way she has," he mumbled.

Marvin grinned knowingly. "Got you by the balls, huh?" he asked, taking a swig from his beer.

Jack frowned. "Not even Bethany got under my skin like this. Man, I feel like I'm in heaven and hell at the same time."

Marvin laughed, then said, "It's about time, dude, that's all I got to say. Welcome to the real world," lifting his bottle, toasting him.

Jack turned toward the door and there she was, coming in, smiling. He felt his mouth lifting, then grew angry when she turned and talked to the man behind her. He sat down again, heavily. Marvin followed his gaze. "Uh-oh," he said, his voice low.

Jack angrily watched Gillian and a man who looked to be in his late forties go toward the back of the bar. They were talking animatedly, laughing a lot.

"You know that guy?" Marvin asked.

Jack silenced him with a glare.

"'Spose not," Marvin said, facing forward.

Jack sat there, fighting the urge to go smash the guy's face in. She had looked right at him as they passed and acted like she didn't even see him. He ran his hand over his face. He glanced at Marvin who deliberately was ignoring him.

He looked back toward Gillian, watched as she got up, went to the bathrooms at the back. He moved in that direction, waiting in the small alcove for her to exit, wanting to kill her, hurt she would do this to him.

She came out of the bathroom and immediately went to a phone, not seeing him, turning her back as she dug in her purse for a quarter. He came up beside her, stood there staring. She finally raised her eyes, looked at him. Her face seemed harder, more rigid. Her eyes were cold, green marbles.

"Hi," she said, then turned back to the machine.

"You want to tell me what's going on?" Jack asked, his voice low.

She shrugged her shoulders. "Nothing," she said, then gave him a belligerent look. "Nothing at all."

He stood staring at her for a moment, then said, his voice low, "You don't feel the need to explain yourself?"

She gave him an innocent look. "Explain what?" she asked, then smiled.

He could have slapped her. Instead, he put his hands out, grabbed her upper arms, shook her slightly. "Gillian, what the hell is going on with you?" he asked her, his teeth gritted.

Her face instantly changed, softening, looking more like the Gillian he knew. She gave him a dazed look, then confusedly glanced around, her eyes returning to his. If he hadn't known better, he would have thought she had just woken up. "Jack?" she asked softly, as if surprised to see him.

He stared at her.

"Jack, what are you doing here?" she said, looking bewildered.

The man she was with came up to them. "Everything all right here?" he asked, glancing at Jack.

Gillian turned to him. "Uh, yes. Sure. Everything's fine," she said, her voice halting, glancing at Jack and then back to the man.

Jack clinched his fists, then left before he did what they were itching to.

The next day, Jack was sitting at his desk, in a black mood, angrily reliving last night's scene while pretending to be listening to Marvin once more going over the details of Oberman's alibis, when he looked up and saw Gillian standing a short distance away.

She stepped into the homicide section, giving Jack a tentative smile. He stopped when he caught sight of her, glaring, wanting to just get up and leave but, damn it, this was his office, his territory.

Marvin, seeing Jack's glare and Gillian's timorousness, easily reading this situation, abruptly stood up, mumbling, "Well, I've got things to see to," as he headed toward the door. He gave Gillian a sympathetic smile, nodding his head at her as he left.

"What do you want?" Jack asked, his voice cold, not standing as he normally would have, just sitting there, waiting while she approached his desk.

"I need to talk to you, Jack," she replied, her voice cracking.

He didn't indicate yea or nay, just continued to glare.

She came and stood before his desk, like a repentant child.

He was glad no one else was in the room.

"Jack, I'm not here to excuse my behavior," she said, her voice small. "I just want you to understand what happened."

"It seemed pretty obvious to me, what happened," he snapped at her.

She sighed. "I don't blame you for not making this easy on me, but please, Jack, just hear me out, then I'll go." She paused, waiting for his permission, but he remained taciturn. She nodded her head, as if she understood. "I, well, sometimes I do things that don't make sense to me, things I don't even realize I'm doing, actually," she went on. "There's something wrong with me, Jack. I don't know, maybe I'm acting subconsciously or something." Seeing his look, she stopped, then said, her voice low. "I know that doesn't make sense to you, but I don't know how else to explain it. After I saw you last night, I felt so badly. I mean, I don't what I . . ." She shook her head. "Anyway, I've thought about it since then, and I guess I was hoping that you would see me," she said, startling him. "I must have wanted you to see me with him, get mad at me, leave me, get out of my life."

Jack couldn't believe this, was too stunned to speak.

"I love you more than any person I have ever in my life known," she said, her voice strained. "I think I did what I did because I wanted to force you away from me, Jack. It's the only way I knew how."

"Why? If you love me, why would you want me out of your life, Gillian? Damnit, that makes no sense to me!"

"Because I'm scared," she said, her voice small.

"Scared?"

"I'm scared of you," she said, giving him a defiant look.

He gave a derisive laugh. "Scared of me? Give me a break, Gillian. That doesn't ride with me."

She sighed heavily, tears coming to her eyes. "I'm scared of my feelings for you," her voice dropping. He had to lean forward to hear what she said. "I'm scared of the intenseness of our relationship, the depth of my love for you. I feel too vulnerable with you, too out of control."

"Shit, Gillian, you're not feeling anything I haven't," he said, his voice softening.

She gave him a pleading look. "I've never felt this way before, Jack. I should have just come right out and told you, but I just didn't know how without a confrontation. So I guess I set the whole thing up. I knew you'd probably be there last night, and I guess I wanted you to see me. I guess I wanted you to just let me go! But the way you looked at me, the way you acted. I didn't think it would hurt so much. I didn't think losing you would be so devastating to me!" She began to cry then, the tears falling silently down her face.

He sat, watching her, not sure whether to believe her or not. He was still feeling hurt, after all.

"I didn't want it to end, with you angry at me, thinking I had been

121

unfaithful to you. I wasn't. I went home alone, right after you left. I just wanted you to know, Jack, it's not you, it's me. I can't allow myself to be vulnerable. I had to pull myself away. I just did it wrongly." With that, she turned on her heel and left.

He sat there contemplating, fighting the urge to go after her. Got up, kicked his desk, yelling "Shit!" as he did so. Damn, why did she have to pull something like that? Why couldn't she have just talked to him, expressed her feelings to him? He stood looking out the window, watching her as she exited the building into the parking lot, heading toward her car. Kept watching as she got to the car, seemed to be struggling to get it unlocked, then finally gave up, putting her face into her hands, leaning against the car, crying. *Fuck it*, he thought, leaving.

When he approached her, he saw she had pulled a tissue from her purse, was wiping her eyes with one hand, trying to insert her key with the other. He came up to her, touched her back lightly, placing his hand over hers, took the keys from her, said, "Here, Gillian, let me do it," his voice gentle.

She stood there, allowing him to open the door for her, and after he had, sat in the car, turning her face slightly away from his, so he couldn't see her.

He squatted down on his haunches, uncomfortably waited for her to stop crying and look at him.

She breathed deeply, trying to control herself, glanced at him, said, "I'm really sorry for what I did, Jack," and put her hand out to close the door.

His own hand reached out, waylaying her progress, forcing her to face him.

"I'm still mad at you for the way you handled this, Gil," he said, his voice firm, low, "but I'm also glad you love me, that you feel as strongly for me as you do. It means a lot to me that you told me."

She nodded her head.

"I just need to know one thing, Gillian. Are you telling me bye now? Is this what you want, to end our relationship?"

She burst out crying again.

"Oh, Gil," Jack said, getting uncomfortable again.

He couldn't help but notice the curious glances he was receiving from people entering and exiting the building, so heaved himself up, closed her door, went around to the passenger side, knocked with his knuckles on the window for her to unlock the door. She released the door locks. He slid into the seat, turned, gathered her into his arms, breathing in her scent, closing his eyes, thankful she was here.

"I'm just as scared as you are, Gillian," he whispered against her hair, "but I don't want to let you go. I don't think it's what you want, either. So, we'll take it slower, okay? We'll try not to be so, what was the word you used, intense with each other."

She smiled at this, raised her head up, looked into his eyes. "You're such a wonderful man, Jack," she said, giving him an admiring look. "You're truly special. I don't deserve you."

"Honey, you deserve a lot better than this," he said, self-effacingly.

"No, I don't." She gave a little, shaky sigh. "I never really believed love existed, till you," she said, giving him a half smile.

He nodded his head, then, "So, can we still see each other?" trying to make his voice calm.

She hesitated.

"Please," he whispered, the feeling strong in his voice now. "Don't let this stop, Gillian. Please."

She brought her face to his, stared intently at him, then kissed him passionately. "I couldn't stop this, even if I wanted to," she said afterward. "I found that out last night."

"I'm glad," he said, smiling at her.

She cocked her head, giving him an impish grin. "I don't have anything to do this afternoon, darlin. I was just wondering if you could come play with me."

He smiled, then glanced back toward the building. "I've got a lot of work to do, Gil," he said, wishing he didn't.

"You have to take a lunch hour, don't you?" she asked, glancing at her watch. "It's eleven now, can't you take it early? My apartment's only ten minutes from here. I'll bring you back after."

In answer, he pulled his seat belt out, put in on.

She was silent all the way to her place, but would glance at him from time to time, smiling shyly at him.

When they got there, she hurried ahead of him, unlocked her door, held it open for him, and as soon as he was inside, closed it, dropping her purse and keys, pulling him to her, kissing him passionately, tugging him to the floor.

She was frantic with him, kissing him feverishly, making murmuring sounds, moving her hands over his body, undressing him as he undressed her.

Without foreplay, she nudged him onto his back, positioned herself over him, throwing her head back as she settled on him, then began laboring her body, moving it back and forth quickly.

He put his hands on her hips and stopped her. She looked at him. He shook his head at her, rolled over, placing her beneath him, began a slow, rhythmic movement with her, placing his mouth on her breasts. Almost immediately, she stiffened, then cried out. He hesitated, wondering. When he looked at her, there were tears in her eyes.

"Gil?" he asked. "Oh, baby, I didn't hurt you, did I?"

She gave him a contented smile through her tears. "Oh, Jack, it happened!" she said, happily. "It finally happened, and it was with you, it was with who I wanted it to be with."

Knowing he shouldn't be, knowing he wasn't the reason for it, that it was partly biological and partly chemical on her part, Jack still felt proud of himself.

"I'm not broken anymore," she whispered, her mouth against his ear. "You fixed me, Jack, you took away the demons."

He hardly heard her, busy with the feelings raging in his own body.

Later, she insisted they make love again, on the bed this time. "I won't be worth a flip this afternoon," he complained as she led him in that direction, but didn't offer any resistance.

"It's like falling off a horse," she said, lying on the bed, pulling him to her "only in reverse. We have to do it once more to see if it happens again. It won't take long, I promise, and I swear I'll be gentle with you."

He laughed, but not for long, and was pleased when it happened for the second time, but not as pleased as his lover.

Gillian fell asleep almost immediately afterward, telling Jack she was so sated she couldn't stand it, and Jack dozed off, thinking he'd allow himself a ten-minute nap before he got up.

When he awoke, the bed was empty. He raised up, looking around, then glanced at the beside clock, noticing it was now two o'clock. "Shit," he said, getting up, looking for his clothes, remembering they were in the living room.

He walked that direction, then stopped when he saw Gillian sitting Indian-style in the middle of the living room floor, completely nude, his gun in her hands. He stood there, watching her, wondering what the heck she was doing with his gun, as she moved her hands lovingly over the handle, down the barrel, placing it against her cheek, gently rubbing the side of her face with it, then against her breasts and down her abdomen.

"Gil?" he asked, stepping into the room. "What the hell are you doing, Gil?"

She startled at his voice, her hands flying open, the gun dropping to the carpet. "Oh!" she gasped, looking at the weapon lying within her crossed legs.

"Damn, Gil, you ought to know better than to play with guns!" he snapped, going to her, reaching down, picking it up. "What if the safety hadn't been on? It could have gone off, blown your head off, for Pete's sake," he fussed at her.

He stopped, seeing the tears in her eyes, then bent down, said, his voice gentle, "I'm sorry, I didn't mean to yell at you. It's just, I was scared, baby. You could get killed by this thing. What the heck were you doing with it anyway?"

She gave him a flustered look, then said, her voice small, "I don't know, Jack, I must have been sleepwalking or something. I didn't even know I was out here, with that thing," pointing at it, crying now. "I hate guns. I can't imagine what I was doing with it."

"It's okay, honey," he said, putting his arms around her. "You probably were sleepwalking or maybe half-asleep and not aware of what you were doing. It's all right."

"Oh, Jack, I thought this was over," she said, crying.

"What? You thought what was over?" he asked her, drawing back looking at her.

"Not knowing why I do things," she wailed, "losing track of what I'm doing."

"Honey, it's okay," he said. "You were half-asleep, you just weren't aware. We all do that sometimes," trying to comfort himself as well as her.

CHAPTER 19

Dr. Barnard was on the phone with a patient when his inner door burst open and Ronnie stalked into the room. He stopped talking, watching her face as she advanced toward him, feeling fear settling in his stomach and intestines like hot, liquid steel.

She snatched the phone out of his hand, banged it on the receiver. Her face was ugly with fury, her eyes dark and menacing.

"Ronnie, I don't believe this is our regular time," he said, overtly looking at his watch, trying to keep his voice even, trying to establish control.

"You going to throw me out?" she asked him, leaning her face toward his. "You got the balls to try and throw me out of here?"

He drew back, away from her. "I can see something has upset you," he said. "Perhaps you should sit down and talk about it."

"I can see something has upset you," she mimicked him. "Well, duh, doctor! Your profundity is truly amazing!" she snapped.

"Sarcasm will not help this situation," he said, looking her in the eyes, trying not to show how afraid he had become of her since he had begun to treat her.

"You have got to help me and I mean now!" Ronnie screamed at him. "I can't afford for you to drag this on any longer. Things are out of control and I need to be in control, you know that. After all, I am supposed to be the strong one here!" She began to pace back and forth in front of his desk.

The psychologist sat, watching the young woman pacing before him, his hand nervously hovering near the telephone, regretting furiously that he had not signed on with the security agency that had just tried to solicit his business, wishing he had not been so cheap and had invested in the services of a receptionist.

"She's getting stronger," Ronnie ranted, continuing to pace, throwing her arms around. "She confines me now." She turned and stared at him. He noticed spittle at the corners of her mouth. Her eyes were cold, dead pieces of moss-covered flint.

"I think you should try to calm down," he said, indicating the chair in front of his desk with his free hand. "We'll talk this out. Just

126

try to breathe deeply, try to relax, and – "
"You cheap piece of shit!" she raved. "You sit there so ceremoniously pompous and arrogant and you don't know the first thing there is to know about psychology, much less treating anyone with my disorder!" As she came toward him, he drew back, fear evident in his face.

She laughed harshly. "You're even a wimp, you puss-filled douche bag," she ranted.

"Ronnie, this is not going to – "

"You have to help me become the host!" she screamed at him. "She's becoming too strong. If this keeps up, she'll completely do away with me. I can feel it!" She stopped, looked at him, came toward him again. His hand tightened on the receiver. She seemed not to notice.

"She wouldn't let me kill him when I wanted to. She intervened, took control. She keeps stepping in and interfering with my plans for him. Do something, damn you, you idiot!"

His face turned white as he considered what she had just relayed to him. He cleared his throat, then said, "Ronnie, you promised me there would be no more killings. That's the only reason I agreed to continue to treat you, on that condition."

She came closer, her face red, her fists clenching and unclenching. "Have you been reading the papers or do you live in your own little world, Barnard? In case you missed it, I lied, Doctor, and my next victim will be you if you don't help me take control of this body," placing her hands on his desk, leaning toward him, her voice low, threatening. He had to literally force himself not to gasp with terror. He realized with some embarrassment he had to urinate badly.

"You know I can do it," she continued. "I've told you about the others. You may not fit within the parameters I've established for my kills, but by God, I'll do away with you and smile while I watch you die if you don't help me!" She straightened up quickly.

"I can't help you while you're in this condition," he said, his voice low, unsteady. "You have to calm down now."

Ronnie stalked away, then turned back to him. "How in the fuck do you expect me to stay calm when I'm losing control here?" she snapped, her voice low, angry. "It's like she senses me now. Before, she had no idea I was even around, but it's different now, things are different, and I cannot accomplish what I need to unless you completely put me in control and get rid of her. Now, either you help me or this will be the last day you'll spend on this earth, you quasi-Freudian piece of shit."

The psychologist picked up the phone, dialed 911, his hand shaking visibly.

"What the hell are you doing?" Ronnie asked, going toward him.

"I'm calling the police," he said, his voice cracking.

Ronnie leaned forward, disconnected the phone by placing her finger on the cutoff button, then laughed at the expression on his face. "And what would you tell them, dear doctor? You are bound by doctor-patient confidentiality, and you know it."

"Not if I suspect you're going to commit another murder," he said, his voice low, pressured. "Then my responsibility is toward the protection of others, not you."

She straightened up, looking at him, then began laughing. "Oh, you're some piece of work," she said, then sat in the chair. She gave him a cold smile. "All right, I'll calm down. I'll do whatever you say, but I'm warning you, I need your help and you better give it."

"I'll help you if I can," he said, putting the phone down, "but I will not treat you if you continue to commit these atrocities. We've discussed that."

She smirked at him. "Okay, okay, I'll abide by the contract," she finally said.

"Further, if you come in here like this again, threatening me, I will terminate treatment at once."

Ronnie looked at him like he was nuts. "Oh, was I threatening, doctor? I'm so sorry," she said, her voice sarcastic. "I'll be sure and mind my manners next time."

The psychologist glanced at the clock. "That might be a good idea, to hold this off until next time, Ronnie," he said, his voice still shaky with fear. "That will give me a chance to research your problem more, try to come up with a better way to hurry this process up for you. Besides, I have a patient due in a few minutes."

Ronnie rose from the chair, pointed her finger at him, and said, "You better not be trying to placate me or buying time, Buster Brown, 'cause the next time I walk into this office, I better walk out as Ronnie and only Ronnie, you got that?" she said, putting her face within inches of his own.

"I fully understand what you're saying," Dr. Barnard replied, watching with relief as she left his office without saying anything else.

After he heard the front door close, he picked up the phone, dialed 911.

CHAPTER 20

Jackson was sitting at his desk, going over the files for the zillionth time, it seemed, trying to find some buried lead, when his phone rang.

"Daniels," he answered, his voice curt.

"Um, uh, I," a man started, then cleared his voice. "I believe I have some information concerning the serial murders that have been occurring recently."

"Yeah?" Jack asked, bored already, wondering what crazy story this guy had.

The man cleared his throat again, and when he spoke, his voice was stronger.

"My name is Dr. Larry Barnard. I'm a psychologist here in Knoxville. As you may not be aware, due to doctor-patient confidentiality, I am bound by my profession not to reveal any information I might have as to past murders committed by a patient." He paused, then went on. "However, if I believe there is danger to someone in the future, shall we say, along the same lines as what I have been told, I would be bound to report that to the police."

Jack frantically snapped his fingers at Marvin, indicating for him to pick up.

"Are you saying you think you're treating the person who is committing these killings?" Jack asked, watching Marvin's face.

"What I'm saying is I cannot relay any of that information. However, I do believe there is going to be another one and I do believe I am treating the person who will be committing the, um, atrocity, if you will."

There was silence while Jack and Marvin stared at each other, contemplating this.

"Can you give me a name?" Jack asked, his voice low, drawing a pad toward him.

"I'm afraid there's not very much I can give you, but I will certainly pass on what I can."

Jack noticed the psychologist's voice sounded relieved. "You wouldn't believe how horrible this has been, hearing all these things

I've been told about the murders right from the mouth of . . ." He stopped.

"Go on," Jack encouraged.

"I'm sorry, I thought I heard someone opening the front door," Dr. Barnard said. He laughed lightly. "I've been hearing a lot of nonexistent things lately," he admitted.

"Anything you can tell us will help, Doctor," Jack prodded.

There was a pause, then Barnard said, "I do have a name for you, as well as an address, although I believe the name I've been given is not the real name of the person you're looking for. However, I can describe that person for you, but I would like to speak with you in person, not relay this information over the phone." Dr. Barnard gave an embarrassed chuckle. "I'm afraid I've become somewhat paranoid since I came into this information. I feel as though someone is watching and listening at all times."

"I understand," Jack said, then, "Tell me where you are and I'll come to you," picking up a pencil, ignoring Marvin's frantic hand motions in his direction.

The doctor gave his address.

"My partner and I will be there within fifteen minutes," Jack said, rising, grabbing for his jacket.

"I'll be waiting," Barnard replied, then added, "Please hurry," before hanging up.

Marvin drove like a madman, siren bleeping if someone too slow was in front of them, toward the professional building complex in West Knoxville which housed the psychologist's office, chastising Jack over and over for not making the doctor give them the information over the phone, which Jack neglected to respond to.

"Well, at least we finally got a break in this case," Marvin observed, tired of Jack ignoring him, turning into the office complex.

Jack leaned forward, squinting. "That looks like Gillian's car," he said, watching a dark green Saturn which had exited the complex traveling away from them in the opposite direction. The vehicle was too far away to make out the license plate.

"No, man, that girl had dark hair, that wasn't your woman," Marvin said, turning into the lot and parking the car. He glanced at Jack. "Shit, man, can't you think of nothing else these days?" he chided, which Jack chose to ignore.

"You know how these things usually turn out," Jack grumbled, getting out of the car, looking at Marvin.

"Yeah, some nutcase wanting his 15 minutes of fame," Marvin said.

The door to the psychologist's office was open, and they stepped into a small, empty reception area.

"You feel that?" Marvin asked, glancing at Jack.

"Back of your neck crawling?" Jack said, his voice low.

Marvin drew his gun. "Something ain't right, man."

Jack followed suit, then opened the inner door, which he presumed would lead to the doctor's office, holding his gun pointed toward the ceiling. He peered cautiously in, then, "Oh, shit!" he raved.

Marvin went past him, approached the man slumped back in his chair behind the desk, reached out tentatively toward the neck for a pulse, but seeing all the blood, the eyes rolled back in his head, drew back.

"He's dead, no way a man could be alive, losing that much blood," Marvin said.

"Damn!" Jack ranted.

They stood staring at who they presumed to be Dr. Barnard, whose throat had been slashed from ear to ear, creating a large, gaping second mouth in his neck. There was a huge puddle of blood on the desk in front of the doctor, spray on the carpet in front of the desk.

"Damn!" Jack repeated, pacing back and forth.

"Man, how many times I got to tell you, when they offer to give a name, don't wait on it. You should have made him tell you over the phone," Marvin said.

"How was I supposed to know this was going to happen?" Jack said. "Shit, man, this is like something out of a bad movie," he snarled, going behind the doctor, looking on his desk.

"Hey," he said.

"What?" Marvin asked, joining him.

"Is that something under his hand there, something he wrote?" Jack asked, pointing.

"Can't tell man, there's too much blood," Marvin said.

They looked at each other.

"I won't tell we moved the body if you don't," Marvin said.

Jack reached out, got a pencil, used it to scoot the dead man's hand away from the large blotter on his desk.

It looked like he had tried to write the letters R, O and then something like a small, undotted I with his own blood in the lower right-hand corner of the blotter.

"Talk about leaving behind a clue," Marvin said, his voice soft.

"What's that third letter, you think?" Jack asked.

Marvin studied it a moment. "I don't know, start of an I, maybe. T? Hell, could be anything, D, H, N, R."

"Okay, R-O," Jack said. "Could be first name, last name, who knows." They looked at each other.

"R-O, as in Ronnie," Marvin said.

"As in we had the damn killer right in our fucking hands and let him go."

"We got to call this in," Marvin said, "get Bogie out here."

"Yeah, but what's a few minutes gonna hurt?" Jackson asked, pulling on rubber gloves, then opening the file drawer beside the desk.

"Those files are confidential," Marvin said, watching Jack shuffle through the contents.

"We'll just check the ones starting with R-O," Jackson said. He looked at Marvin. "Listen, if we can, we need to rule in or rule out Ronnie, okay, and as fast as possible.

Marvin didn't look like he was buying it.

"Look, guy, I swear to you anything I find in any of these files that does not relate to our case, I will not divulge to anyone, okay?" Jack said. "I know this is all confidential, but do you know how long it would take to get a warrant allowing us to take a look at this shit? We'd have to go through the guy's attorney, executor, administrator, and God for all I know before we could even take a small peek. Not to mention, we'd probably have to get permission from each and every patient in here. Why not now, before anyone else gets here, just you and me, no one else. I trust you, you trust me. We'll get what we need and no one will ever be the wiser as to how we got it, okay? We'll only look at the data sheet, ascertain the age and sex, make sure it meets our profile before we take it any further."

Marvin looked doubtful.

"Hey, man, this is our first true break in this case," Jack prodded. "You gonna let this one get out from under us because some asshole's written some stupid law forbidding us to investigate in order to protect our murderer's rights and screw the guys getting mutilated?" Jack asked.

"Five minutes," Marvin said, donning his own rubber gloves.

They found three patients starting with R-O. One was a preadolescent girl, one was a woman 63 years of age, and the third was a man 32 years old. They pulled that file, took a quick gander then put it back when they read the man was a paraplegic.

"Damnit to hell!" Jack yelled, slamming the file drawer shut.

Marvin noticed the computer on the psychologist's credenza, went toward it. "Wait a minute," he said. "If our killer was here, chances are he/she took their file, wouldn't you think, in order to protect their ass?"

Jack nodded.

Marvin turned on the computer. "Okay, it took us, what, minus fifteen minutes to get here. Would our killer have had enough time to kill the good doctor, pull his or her file, then go into the computer?"

Jack grinned. "If Herr Doctor kept any info in there on his patients, we just might hit pay dirt," he said.

"Hey, man, am I good or what?" Marvin asked, watching the menu come up.

"Never said otherwise," Jack said, watching Marvin play with the keyboard. He found a listing of patients, scrolling down to those beginning with R. "This one says Ronnie, no last name," Marvin said, pointing.

"See if you can pull it up," Jack suggested.

"You think we'll ever get used to that smell?" Marvin asked, looking around at the bloody corpse.

"Hell, I hope not," Jack answered.

"Here we go," Marvin said, as words flashed onto the screen. It appeared to be a listing of dated notes under the caption "Ronnie."

"Says, 'Ronnie, no last name. Presents 10-15.'"

Jack looked at Marvin. "That was right after the first one."

Marvin nodded. "Look here, Marvin," Jack said, pointing.

"Same address as the courthouse," Marvin said, then, "Damnit to hell!"

"Same address given by each and every victim so far," Jack muttered.

"Shit man, no last name, no address, what the fuck good is that gonna do us?"

"'Claims MPD'" Jackson read. He looked back at Marvin. "What's that?"

"Hell, man, you're the one was married to a psychiatrist, you tell me."

They looked back at the screen.

"'Claims to be the alternate personality,'" Marvin read. "What the hell?" he asked looking at Jack.

Jack nodded his head, getting it. "MPD, Multiple Personality Disorder, a really good copout for the evil-minded serial killer."

"You mean we ain't gonna see this baby fry?" Marvin said.

Jack started reading again. "'Does not want to merge with host but instead become the primary personality. Seems to feel the host can be disposed of in some way.'"

"Huh!" Marvin said.

Jack raised up. "Can we print this thing out?" he asked Marvin.

"Sure," he replied, his hands going to the keyboard again.

They watched the printer spit the notes out, then Jack picked the paper up.

"There's not much more on here," Jack said, then continued reading: "'Actual DID . . .'"

"DID?" Marvin interrupted.

"Yeah, Dissociative Identity Disorder, I think that's the new term nowadays." He continued. "'Actual DID or simply alleging to be? Possesses inflated sense of self. Suffers from narcissism. Seems to feel some sort of power. Very sexualized persona. Wonder if host personality, if there actually is one, is as lascivious.'"

"Sexualized, hell, I could have told him that one," Marvin said.

They went back to the notes. Marvin began reading this time. "'Promises to cease with killings, agrees to contract that condition.'"

Jack, who was reading ahead, interrupted, "We just got the confirmation, Marvin, look here," pointing with his finger.

Marvin read, "'Claims writes the name of abusive father on wall behind dead body with dead man's blood.'" They looked at each other again.

"Man, I am having a hard time believing this shit," Marvin said, his voice low.

"We better call Bogie," Jack said.

"What are we gonna do with this printout?" Marvin asked.

Jack thought. "The address on here is bogus, we actually got nothing," he said, waving the paper. "No info other than the name Ronnie. Hell, this doesn't give us much to go on." He folded it, put it in his back pocket. "This is between us," Jack said, looking at Marvin.

"There's one thing," Marvin said.

"What's that?"

"Chances are looking pretty good it may be our guy," Marvin answered. "How we going to convince the Sarge we know it's him?"

Jack looked at him. "If we tell them that, we'll have to tell them how we got that information."

"Damn!" Marvin spouted. He paced back and forth, then looked at Jack. "You know we could lose our badges over this," he said, his voice low.

Jack thought. "Unless I tell them Dr. Barnard told me when he called that the killer's name is Ronnie," Jack said.

Marvin looked at him.

"Look, guy, I got you into this, I won't drag you any further. Besides, he did tell me, in an indirect way," pointing at the computer.

Marvin went over, turned it off. "Make the call," he said, glancing at the dead psychologist.

After Jack had called in the crime scene investigative team, he and Marvin stepped out of the office and waited in the reception area. They peeled the rubber gloves off, stuffed them in their back pockets.

Marvin looked around, noticing the chairs against three of the walls, one low coffee table sporting magazines, a wilted fichus tree in the corner. There was no area for a receptionist, or phone.

"You reckon he didn't use a receptionist?" Marvin asked.

Jack glanced around, then shrugged. "Probably not. Bethany just uses a device that goes off when the front door opens, signaling someone's in the outer area. She says it's a whole lot cheaper than paying someone by the hour to sit and make nice with the patients. Her words. I think a lot of these people do that nowadays."

Marvin nodded his head.

Bogie was first to arrive after the EMT and Jack explained to him the call he had received from the psychologist and what they had found when they arrived.

"You touch anything?" Bogie asked, studying Jack.

Jack and Marvin looked at each other.

"Damn!" Bogie said.

"We haven't altered the evidence in any way," Jack said, giving Bogie an intent look. "We wouldn't do that, Boge."

Bogie nodded his head, stepped around them and into the inner office after the paramedics confirmed the doctor was dead.

Jack and Marvin stood in the doorway, watching the crime scene specialists work the room, searching for evidence.

They were surprised when their sergeant spoke behind them.

"What kind of crap you two stepped into now?" he boomed, causing Jack to startle.

"You know about the call Jack got?" Marvin asked.

"Yeah, Robin overheard you two when you were heading out the door, then when Bogie got called over here, I figured something was rotten."

Jack nodded his head. "The victim claimed he was the psychologist treating the perp we've been looking for," he said, waving his hand toward the dead man still slumped back in his chair.

McKinley glanced that way. "Shit-fire," he said, his voice low, then, "I assume he was dead when you got here."

"Yep," Marvin said.

"He tell you anything over the phone?" the sergeant asked.

Jack fought the urge to look at Marvin. "He told me, before Marvin got on the line, that he had been treating our serial killer. He said he had been given a name by this person, although he didn't think that was the killer's actual name."

Sergeant McKinley nodded his head. "And did you get the name?" he asked.

"All he had to give me was the name Ronnie," Jack answered, trying not to sweat.

"Ronnie? As in your transvestite, Ronald Oberman," McKinley mused. He looked at Jack.

"The only problem is, this guy's alibis have checked out so far,"

Marvin said, looking at Jack. "Either he's legit, or he's got people covering his ass pretty tight."

"You got anything else?" McKinley asked.

"Nope," Jack answered, glancing at Marvin.

"Not much to go by," Marvin said.

"Not much at all," McKinley agreed. He looked around, then said, "Well, I guess I better go call the mayor. It ain't gonna make my job any easier trying to explain this situation."

"You don't have to give them this one," Jack said, tilting his head in the general direction of the corpse. "It doesn't fit the MO, the media doesn't have to know he was the one treating the perp."

The sergeant thought, then said, "But, dear boy, if I don't spin this one and word gets out, I am fucked." He headed toward the phone, then turned back to them. "As soon as you leave here, I think it might be wise to go track down our Ronnie and bring him in for questioning, see what kind of alibi he can provide us for this one."

"Well, I guess I'll get them rookies standing around outside to see if they can come up with any possible witnesses," Marvin said, going toward the exit, then looked back at Jack. "Like we'll find any," he finished, sounding despondent, then went out the door.

Robin came in, her face flushed. She stomped up to Jack. "I really appreciate being left out of this," she said, sounding angry.

"Robin, I'm sorry," Jack said, meaning it. "We got the call and I was in such a rush to get here to talk to this guy, I didn't even notice you were in the room." He looked toward the dead man. "As if it did us any good," he finished, watching the technicians.

"Another dead end?" she asked.

Jack nodded his head, then ran his hands through his hair. "All we got was the name Ronnie."

"The transvestite?" she asked.

Jack nodded his head.

"He's not the one, Jack. We checked his alibis inside and out, and so far he's pretty legit. Besides, I don't think he fits the protocol for something like this."

Jack looked back at Robin, who was watching the scene inside.

"Robin, there's something I've been wanting to talk to you about," he said, his voice low.

She turned back to him.

"This probably isn't the right time, but I've been wanting to say this for a long time, and it seems there never is a good time, really." She watched him, waiting.

"About what happened, between us, I know it's caused some hard feelings. I just wanted to explain that I didn't mean to hurt you or make you feel bad. We were really good friends before, good partners, and I'd like to get back to what we were then, not now." She cocked her head at him. "Jeez, Jack, what's got you so soft all of a sudden?"

He frowned at her.

"Okay, I'm sorry," she said, reading his look. "I'm just not used to apologies from you."

"Yeah, well, I owe you one big time," he said.

"Go ahead, then," Robin answered, "I won't stop you."

Jack looked at her, gauging her sincerity, then continued, "Even though I wanted badly to sleep with you, I didn't want to because I knew it would change things between us. Surely you knew that, Robin, and when we actually did sleep together, I knew I had really fucked up bad. I didn't feel like I could be your friend and lover too, you know. I knew it would affect the way we worked together, so I left the way I did that night, you know, afterwards without saying anything, because I was feeling that. To tell you the truth, I wanted you more as a partner than a lover. Not that the lover part wasn't nice, but I just don't think two cops who work so closely together need to be that intimate, if you can understand what I'm trying to say here."

Robin surprised him by smiling. "You know, I was thinking along those same lines, too," she said.

He stared at her.

"Yeah, just like you. Gee, Jack, think of all the bad feelings we could have saved if we had just talked about this then," she said.

"Go figure," he replied, causing her to laugh.

"Friends," he asked, putting his hand out.

"And partners," she answered, shaking with him.

McKinley came up, "All right, stop making out and get to work, you two," causing them to grin at each other.

Jack went to find Marvin. "You ready to go talk to our orthodontist?"

Marvin consulted his watch. "Still office hours, you want to go there first?"

Jack nodded his head.

When they got to Oberman's office, the waiting area was deserted. They approached the receptionist behind the glass partition, both producing their badges for her perusal. She rose, opened the glass partition. "Can I help you?" she asked, smiling at Marvin, with whom she had talked before.

Marvin took the time to smile back, then asked, "Is Dr. Oberman in, Sara?"

She shook her head. "No, he's not. He and his wife took their kids to the beach. They've been gone a week now. He should be here Monday, though."

Jack and Marvin looked at each other, both thinking the same thing: the guy had left without asking permission to.

"Have you talked to him since he left?" Jack asked.

"Oh, yes. He calls every day. Even though he's not here, we still have technicians who can handle some of the work while he's away, you know, adjustments, things like that, and he likes to be kept abreast of everything while he's away."

"And you're sure he's calling from – where did you say he was?" Jack asked.

"Hilton Head, South Carolina," she answered. "Yes, he calls in long distance every day."

"Do you have the number he's at?" Jack asked.

"Sure, I'll get it for you," she said, turning away.

Marvin looked at Jack. "We'll need to get the phone records from here, check all the incoming calls."

"Yeah, but maybe his wife's making those calls for him," Jack said, then shrugged. "Hell, even if he is the one calling in, he could have driven over, you know, it's only what, eight hours or so from here?"

"Shit," Marvin said, his voice low.

"There's just too many open holes in this guy's alibis," Jack said.

"I know, I know," Marvin agreed. "Although, I got to tell you, he don't feel like the one, Jack."

"Yeah, Robin said the same thing," Jack answered, then turned his attention to the receptionist.

After she gave him the number, he asked if he could use their phone to try to get in touch with Dr. Oberman.

He let the phone ring ten times in Dr. Oberman's suite before replacing the call to the hotel he was staying at, asking to speak to the front desk. When the desk clerk came on, he asked if Dr. Oberman had been in that day.

"I haven't seen him, sir, but that doesn't mean he hasn't been here. Just a moment." Jack waited, listening to elevator music, and then the clerk was back. "He has messages in his box which he hasn't picked up, so I take it he's been out most of the day."

"Thanks," Jack said and hung up.

He turned to Sara, whom he noticed was eavesdropping. "Have you talked to Dr. Oberman at all today?" he asked.

"Yes, he called this morning, around nine," she answered.

"Does he call that time every day?" Jack asked.

"No, sir, it varies, but he usually calls in the afternoons."

Jack nodded, then fished out a card. "If Dr. Oberman calls in after we leave, I want you to tell him I need him to get in touch with me immediately, it's very important."

"Certainly," Sara said, giving Jack a questioning look.

Jack and Marvin headed out. In the car, Jack said, "I think we need to call Hilton Head PD and get someone over there to see if they can locate our good doctor and try to ascertain if he's actually been there all day."

"Want to bet he's got that covered, too?" Marvin asked, starting the car.

CHAPTER 21

Jack was sitting in McKinley's office with Marvin, feeling despondent. They had just gotten through with a conference call to a detective in Hilton Head, South Carolina who had been checking out Ronald Oberman's whereabouts on the day of Dr. Barnard's murder. It seemed the guy had a zillion people willing to testify they had seen him at various times that day.

Jack shifted restlessly. Marvin and the Sarge looked at him. "I'm wondering if maybe we're not dealing with a cop here," he said, looking uncomfortable.

Everyone was silent.

"I mean, this killer is too clean, seems to know way too much about what to do to keep from leaving any sort of evidence behind."

Marvin nodded his head in agreement.

"But," the sarge said, leaning forward, "all you got to do to learn the proper way to commit a murder and not leave any evidence is watch cable TV or read a book."

"Or the internet," Marvin said. "You can find out all kinds of junk on the internet."

McKinley sighed, drawing their attention. "Boys, I pray to God we're not dealing with a cop, 'cause if we are, we're never gonna catch the son of a bitch."

Jack turned to his partner. "You told the sarge about your theory yet?" he asked.

"What theory?" McKinley asked.

"Go ahead," Jack encouraged. "At this point, anything seems feasible."

Marvin moved restlessly in the chair. "Well, I was just throwing out an idea to Jack one day that seeing as how these dudes getting themselves offed are of the legal persuasion, which as we all know is notorious for philandering, maybe there's some sort of wive's club out there, takes care of a husband who's, you know, straying from the barn, so to speak."

"Wasn't there a movie about that?" McKinley asked.

Jack and Marvin both shrugged. "I don't get much of a chance to go to the movies," Jack said.

They all thought a moment.

"Anyway," Marvin said, "looks like each of these guys was fooling around maybe where they weren't supposed to be and – "

"Well, not the third one, the divorce attorney," McKinley interrupted.

Marvin nodded his head. "Yeah, well, that probably makes my whole theory moot," he agreed.

"Maybe, maybe not," Jack said. "He was still married, the divorce wasn't final yet. Or could be he was in a serious relationship, you know, maybe on the verge of marriage to someone who found out he wasn't being faithful."

"I think Robin checked that out and the guy was known to be a notorious womanizer, according to her," Marvin said.

"How would something like that work anyway?" McKinley asked. Marvin shrugged.

"The internet," Jack said. "All kinds of services are offered on the internet, you know."

"It's something to think about," McKinley said, not sounding too thrilled about it.

They were doing just that when Robin burst into the room. She looked happy.

"I've found someone who looks just like that woman on the videotapes," she said, smiling at them.

They all three straightened up, staring expectantly at her.

"I've been dating this guy from vice," she explained, her voice pressured. "I was telling him about this woman we've seen in two of the videotapes, the one with the trench coat and dark hair. Well, as it turns out there's a prostitute who works the Old City and he says that's how she usually dresses, trench coat, sunglasses even at night, has dark hair." She gave them a quick grin, then said, "He claims she wears nada under the trench coat." She stopped to get her breath.

"And. . ." McKinley prodded.

"And tonight, Tom and I – that's the guy I'm dating – we went down to the Old City and kind of hung out, and sure thing, there she was. She looks exactly like the woman in the videos."

Jack and Marvin looked at each other.

"You question her?" McKinely asked.

"Nope. Thought I'd run this by you guys, see what you wanted to do first," Robin said. "We've had such bad luck with this case, I want to do it right."

Jack looked at McKinely. "Well?" he asked.

McKinley thought a minute. "Think we'll scare her off if we question her?" he asked.

"One thing you ought to know," Robin said.

They turned to her once more.

"Tom says this woman's got a violent streak a mile wide. Said she's been arrested more than once for assault."

McKinley raised his eyebrows at this. "That's good," he said. "A record, something we can look at."

"Yeah, but, according to Tom, nobody knows her true identity," Robin added. "Says she gives them a different name each time she gets arrested, won't give them any prior addresses. Has no true ID they've ever seen. No fingerprints to match up to any legitimate person."

"She from around here?" Jack asked.

Robin grinned wider, shaking her head no. "Tom says she showed up here around six months ago. She's been arrested three times for assault and battery. Each time, she claimed her victim was assaulting her and it was self-defense."

"She got a pimp?" Marvin asked.

"Strictly self-employed," Robin said. "She's more attractive than most of those girls down there, and she sure don't look like she's hurting for business, from what I observed tonight."

They all thought.

"We could put surveillance on her," Jack suggested.

"Yeah, but how can we justify that cost?" McKinley countered. "Only thing to tie her in is the way she dresses matches a woman on two of the video tapes."

"Plus her propensity for beating up on johns," Marvin said.

They all thought some more.

Jack looked at Robin. "Can you get this Tom to bring her in?" he asked.

She shrugged her shoulders. "We could send out a decoy, get her to solicit him, pull her in that way. Only thing is, Tom says she's smart as a whip and can scent a law official a mile off. They haven't been able to get her on solicitation so far. She sniffs them out every time."

McKinely, Jack, and Robin turned to look at Marvin. He gave them a startled look, then shook his head no. "Nuh-uh, no way, I ain't gonna go out there and try to tangle myself up with no prostitute, especially one sounds as violent as this one."

Jack grinned. "What happened to the Marvin Mo-Chine?" he chided. "What happened to the connoisseur of women, the guy who–"

"Shut your mouth," Marvin snapped.

"Come on, Marv," Robin said. "You don't look like a cop, you don't act like a cop. You know you don't fit the profile. Chances are, she won't pick up on you, guy."

Marvin thought about it.

"It's decided then," McKinley said. "We'll wire Marvin up, get her to solicit him, get her in here, find some way to question her, see if she knows anything about the murders, try not to get her suspicious enough to cut and run on us."

Later that night, Jack and Robin were inside a used book store across the street from where their prostitute was standing on the corner, waiting for action.

They watched as Marvin drove slowly by in his wife's Taurus, seeming to check the woman out, then circle around the block and come back, this time slower, bending down, peering at her through the passenger side window, mumbling to himself the whole time.

"Coming in for the kill," Robin said beneath her breath.

"Oh, he's a cool one, he is," Jack said, grinning, wondering if Marvin had told his wife what he was up to this evening.

They watched as Marvin stopped the car, rolled down the passenger side window, then listened through their earpieces.

"Hey, girl, what's shakin'?" Marvin asked the woman, who approached the car.

She leaned down, looked in, and they heard her answer, "Not much, man. Just standing around, looking at the scenery."

"Well, what I'm looking at is just about the best scenery I reckon I've set my eyes on in years," Marvin responded, causing Robin to snicker.

The woman leaned into the car. "So, you looking for a little companionship?" she asked, her voice low, sexy.

"Maybe, just very well might be," Marvin answered. "You think you might be able to help me out with that?"

"Shit, watch what you're saying," Jack mumbled. He looked at Robin. "Entrapment," he explained. She nodded, then bent her head down, pressing the earpiece to her ear to hear better.

They heard the woman ask Marvin, "You a cop?" sounding suspicious.

"Damnit," Robin exploded.

Jack held his hand up, signaling her to quiet down.

"Baby, do I look like a cop to you?" Marvin asked, sounding defensive. Jack rolled his eyes. "But if you just so happen to see one anywhere near, I'd appreciate it if you'd let me know 'cause I understand they're looking for me," Marvin added, looking around suspiciously.

"They are?" the prostitute asked. "What'd you do?" leaning further into the car, causing her back to arch, her butt to rise. Robin nudged Jack, grinning.

"Just beat up on some old boy who was beating up on me. Only I did it better," Marvin answered, sounding boastful.

The woman laughed.

"So, baby, you think you might want to go for a ride or something?" Marvin asked.

"What kind of ride we talking about?"

Marvin laughed lecherously. "Well, I reckon that's probably up to you, baby, you get my drift."

She stepped back, pulled open the car door, leaned in again. "It's gonna cost you," she said, her voice low. Jack frowned, barely catching that.

"Yeah?" Marvin asked. "Well, I ain't hurtin' for money, I might could help you out a little."

"Wrong response," Robin muttered.

The woman was quiet. "Uh-oh," Robin said.

"You are one fine-looking woman," Marvin said appreciatively, prompting the woman to say something.

"Better than these other cunts out here," the woman said, her voice low, then, "it'll cost you a hundred for a hand job, two for a blow job, three if you want to fuck," sounding just like what she was. "Anything kinky, price doubles."

Marvin didn't respond right off. "What the hell's he doing?" Jack asked the air.

"How about a trip round the world, how much you charge for that?" Marvin finally asked.

"Shit!" Jack raved. "Signal the others, get them on her before he says something even stupider!"

"Darlin, that takes some time and my time is valuable," the woman was answering, then hesitated and said, "five hundred, I'll take you places you ain't never been before, baby."

"Sounds good to me," Marvin said.

She got into the car. "In advance," she said, holding out her hand.

They watched as Marvin pulled out his wallet, counted the money out, gave it to her, then placed his left arm out the driver's window, giving the signal.

Robin and Jack both breathed a sigh of relief as they watched the officers running toward the prostitute, open the door, grab her, haul her out of the car, then handcuff her.

"Well, our boy did it," Robin said, removing her earpiece.

"Ain't he a natural?" Jack asked.

They grinned at each other.

By the time they got to the station, McKinley had their suspect in a room, sitting, sweating it out, hopefully.

They found Marvin in McKinley's office, crowing over his success.

Robin went up to him, gave him a series of high fives. "See, guy, I told you you didn't have the cop smell on you," Robin said, congratulating him. "You the man!"

Marvin grinned widely at her. "It wasn't that what did it, girl, it was this marvelous body of mine," he answered. "She just couldn't resist the chance to go at it with somebody with my great physique."

"Great bullshit is more like it," Jack said. "And besides, what's the deal with asking her how much to go round the world?" Jack asked irritably. "You just might have blown the whole thing with that one question, you idiot!"

"Hey, I was just curious, just wondering, you know."

Robin and Jack looked at him.

"What?" Marvin asked, giving them an innocent look back.

"Okay," McKinley interrupted, coming into the room. "Who wants to handle this?"

"I do," Jack said.

"I don't reckon she's gonna feel up to talking to me, so I'll just watch," Marvin said.

"I want to sit in on this, Jack," Robin said.

"Let's do it," he answered, opening the door.

CHAPTER 22

Jack went into the interrogation room with the mirrored wall, sat down across from the prostitute, took the time to study her up close. He couldn't help but appreciate the way she looked, even with the sunglasses on.

"You don't look like the average prostitute we get in here," he mused.

"Who said I was a prostitute?" the woman asked belligerently.

"You got more style, more class, a better body."

The woman smiled at this.

"I mean, I'd put you, I don't know, in some high-class hotel, you know, exclusive escort service, something like that, a woman with your looks."

"I'm only working that street corner so I can build my clientele up," she said, then realized her mistake, sitting back, giving Jack a sullen look.

Jack nodded his head. "Won't take you long to do that, looks like," he said.

She kept quiet.

"You work exclusively for yourself or you working the streets for somebody else?" he asked.

"I work hard for my money and I ain't about to share it with nobody else," the woman said, her voice hard. "I'm an independent," she added, acting proud.

"Makes sense to me," Jack said, then, "Any reason you wear sunglasses at night?" he asked her, pulling out a pack of cigarettes, offering her one.

She took it, put it to her mouth, waited for him to light it, took the time to take a drag before answering.

"I have sensitive eyes, any kind of light hurts them. These glasses are specially made."

"Yeah? Who prescribed them?" Jack asked, sitting back, blowing smoke, thinking they might get a legitimate name that way.

"Baby, I don't reckon I remember that," she answered.

"Get 'em here in Knoxville?" he asked, trying to sound

149

disinterested.

"No, sir, got them someplace else, although to tell you the truth, I don't really remember where I got these things, it's been so long." She smiled at him.

Jack nodded. "You mind taking them off?" he asked her.

"Yes, sir, I do," she answered.

"What about the trench coat, I hear that's the way you dress, any reason for that?" he asked, curious.

She sat up, placed the cigarette in the side of her mouth, squinting at the smoke spiraling up, untied the belt, took her time undoing the buttons, then opened the coat, exposing herself to Jack. He took his time looking before saying, "It's a downright shame you have to keep those babies covered up," glancing at Robin, who was turning her head to hide her grin.

The woman laughed, then shrugged, pulling the coat back together. "Makes things easier if I got some dude wants a quickie," her voice sounding street-hard.

Jack nodded his head, as if he understood. "That a wig you're wearing?" he asked.

She smiled. "You tell me," she replied.

Jack studied it, then shrugged. "If it is, it looks real good, real natural."

She put her hands to her hair, primping, then said, "Yeah, it's a wig. Made from real human hair, though."

Jack glanced at the mirror.

"Uh-oh," she said, catching that. "Looks like I might have stepped in some doo-doo with that."

Jack grinned, shook his head no.

"Listen, you got me in this room for a reason, and I know it's not solicitation. If that was the charge, I'd already be out of this joint," she said, her voice growing hard.

Ignoring that, Jack said, "You mind telling us your name?"

"Honey, my name is whatever you want it to be," she cooed at him.

"You got a name I can call you?" Jack asked, watching the woman finish buttoning the trench coat.

"How 'bout Jane Doe? That one always serves me well," she answered, smiling again.

"You know, you remind me of someone," Robin interjected, looking interested.

The prostitute perked up, then said, "Yeah, people tell me I favor that actress on that TV show, you know, one got canceled awhile back, 'Veronica's Closet'? Kirstie Alley's her name."

Jack glanced at the mirror when she said "Veronica," thinking, *Ronnie for short*, then thinking, *Geez, all of a sudden we got all these Ronnies running around.*

"Uh-oh," the prostitute said, catching his look.

"Is that your name, Veronica?" Robin asked.

"If that's what you want it to be, darlin'," the prostitute replied.

Jack stubbed his cigarette out, then leaned toward her. "You hungry, thirsty? Can I get you something to drink, a coke, coffee?"

The woman shook her head no, then consulted her watch. "Honey, I'm losing valuable time here, so I suggest you get on with it. Time is money to me, you know."

Jack wondered if there was any way Bogie could match a hair from her wig to the one found at the crime scene. He leaned toward her. "You mind if we take a hair from your wig, use it for comparison purposes?"

"To what?" she asked, giving him a suspicious look.

Jack shrugged his shoulders, then said, "You greatly resemble a witness seen at a crime scene. We just want to determine if that witness was actually you."

"What crime scene?" she asked, looking from Robin to Jack, then said, "You telling me I'm a suspect? Maybe I need a lawyer here. You-all ain't even advised me of my rights, so I suggest you do that and either tell me what the hell you think I'm guilty of or I'm walking out that door. I don't have to stay here, you know."

"Well, actually, we do have you on the solicitation charge," Robin said, "so I don't guess you'll be going anywhere."

"Then get me a lawyer," the prostitute demanded. "You want to cut a deal with me, think maybe I was a witness to something, you go ahead, do it; otherwise, give me my phone call."

Jack was thinking if they kept her on the solicitation charge, maybe he could get one of the female officers to do a strip search, surreptitiously take a hair from the wig, get it to Bogie, see if he could match it up with the hair found at the crime scene. But could they do that without her permission? Of course not, at this point. And if they did, it wouldn't stand up in a court of law as evidence. Still, a way to preliminarily rule her in or out. If they charged her with solicitation, chances were she'd be gone by the morning, so they needed to do it now. He got up, said, "Excuse me a minute, ma'am," and left the room.

When he got outside, he asked Marvin to track down Bogie, then told him what he was thinking. McKinley, who had been watching through the mirror along with Marvin, nodded his head, said, "That's good, get Bogie in here. I'll go find a female officer to do the strip search, get the hair for us."

"You think we can hold her?" Jack asked McKinley.

"Sheriff's Department holds suspects as long as seventy-two hours, but they're getting sued right and left for that," McKinley said, thinking. "Probably twenty-four hours tops for solicitation, I'd say. I'll check with the legal department after I get the female officer," and took off down the hall.

Jack stood outside the room, looking through the mirror at the prostitute talking to Robin, thinking how greatly she resembled the woman in the videotapes, but feeling in his gut this wasn't the one. He sighed, went back in, sat down again.

"You get your business done?" the woman asked.

Jack ignored that, then said, "I understand you got a reputation for getting violent with your johns."

She laughed, then said, "Honey, you give me sugar, I'll give you sugar. You give me pain, I'll give you even more pain. I don't put up with no shit from my johns. I'm too good-looking, too much in demand. I don't waste my time with guys who want to beat me and then fuck me. They beat me, they gonna get beat back, it's as simple as that."

"Seems only fair," Jack said.

She smiled at this, then leaned back in her chair, spreading her legs. "You ain't a bad-looking dude," she said, eyeing Jack. "I wouldn't mind doing you, no, siree, I wouldn't." She glanced at Robin. "You see, most of my johns, they're these fat, pot-bellied guys smell like beer, don't even know how to fuck a woman good, to tell you the truth, don't know the first thing about it." She looked back at Jack. "But now, you, big guy, you look like you might have had some practice in that department."

Robin smiled. Jack ignored both of them, pulling out another cigarette, lighting it, then reaching into his pocket, producing four pictures, including Dr. Barnard, laying them out in front of the prostitute.

"You know any of these guys?" he asked, watching her look at the photos, then seeing her eyes widen when they landed on the third one, placed his finger on that one, said, "You know him."

She thought a minute, then said, "Yeah, I done him a couple of times."

"Know who he was?" Jack asked.

She shook her head no. "Just another john who wanted me to call him Daddy. I think he told me once he was an attorney, though."

"A divorce attorney," Jack clarified.

She grinned. "Well, darlin, if I'd known that fact, I woulda charged him more."

Jack couldn't help but smile at that. "You remember anything in particular about this guy?" he asked.

She shook her head yes. "Liked to spank," she said. "Liked to use his belt, pretend he was big daddy giving his little girl a spanking." She looked up at Jack, smiling. "But I went along with it. He'd always take me to a nice motel, you know, nice bed, nice carpet, clean. Then afterwards, he'd have a go, and after he got done, he'd give me a nice tip for being so compromising - those were his words - and leave."

Jack noticed Robin was sitting there with her mouth open. He nudged her with his foot. She shut it with a snap.

"You didn't object to him using a belt with you?" Jack asked. "You didn't think he was beating you?"

"Shit no," the prostitute replied. "Hell, honey, half my johns either want to spank me or me to spank them. You guys got something weird going on about that. Now, if he'd used the metal part of the belt, maybe I'd have gotten a little upset. But he wasn't too bad. I could take it." She seemed proud.

Jeez, there's a lot of sick people in this world, Jack thought to himself. "What about the other three, they look familiar to you?" he asked.

She studied the pictures once more. "Nah, can't say as I know

153

them," she finally said.

Jack caught the present tense of her answer, thought a moment, then got up. "Okay, we'll let you have your phone call," he said, going toward the door.

"You ain't even gonna ask me was I the one that did it?" the woman asked as if disappointed.

"Did what?" Jack asked, perking up at that.

"Whatever the hell you think I did," she answered, then laughed. She studied Jack. "Honey, there's only two things I'm good at and that's fucking and beating up on somebody beating up on me. Anything outside of those two areas you're thinking I'm guilty of, you've got the wrong woman."

Jack nodded his head, said, "We'll see," and left.

CHAPTER 23

Jack went back to his office to wait for Bogie. He glanced at the clock, decided he'd try Gillian again. He'd been calling off and on all evening to tell her he'd be late, but she seemed to have forgotten again that they had made plans.

He let the phone ring fifteen times before slamming it down. He tried her cell phone, but only got a recording. He slammed the phone down again.

Marvin came into the room, heard the slam, and noticing Jack's irritated look, said, "What's wrong, your main squeeze ain't where she's supposed to be?"

Jack frowned at him.

"What's up with you?" Marvin asked him, coming over and sitting down across from him. "Hell, man, you've gotten to the point where you can't think of nothing else but that girl all the damn day long." He leaned toward Jack. "She's starting to interfere with your investigative skills, Jack. You're gonna have to get over it, guy, let her be who she is, do what she does, and just realize you can't control her the way it looks like you want to."

"I don't want to control her," Jack said defensively.

"Well, you expect her to be where you can find her twenty-four hours of the day. The girl has a career, you know. She has a life outside of you."

"Hey, Marvin, let me clarify something here," Jack snarled. "First of all, it's none of your frigging business what goes on between me and Gillian, but just for your information, the only thing - and I mean the only thing - I ask from that woman is that she be where she's supposed to be when we're supposed to be having a date! I've been trying all night to call her to tell her I'd be late, and as usual, she's not home for me to tell that to, she's not even answering her damn cell phone. And knowing Gillian, there's no telling where the hell she is," he ranted, getting up, pacing.

"Okay, okay," Marvin said, appeasingly. "Maybe she went out to the store for something, maybe she's in the shower. You got to stop reading things that aren't there, man. You gonna let her tear you apart, you keep this up."

Jack sat back down, ran his hands through his hair. "I know," he said. "Man, I hate this," he added, rubbing his face with his hands.

"Yeah, love do suck sometimes," Marvin said, his voice consoling.

Jack gave him a look. "Aren't you the wise one?"

"Glad to see you back," Marvin said, got up, and went out the door.

Fifteen minutes later, after Jack still hadn't been able to get hold of Gillian, he got up and went down to Bogie's office, finding him at his microscope.

"Well?" Jack asked, standing in the doorway.

Bogie looked up, giving him a frustrated look, shaking his head. "They don't match up," he said. "The one at the crime scene was black, raven colored, our lady of the evening's is more chestnut-colored, more brown than black. There's no way they're from the same wig."

"Shit," Jack said.

"My sentiments exactly," Bogie agreed.

Jack went down the hall to the interrogation room, standing outside watching Robin and their Jane Doe sitting inside chatting away.

He opened the door, went in, caught the prostitute telling war stories.

She looked up at Jack and smiled warmly at him. "I was just telling Robin here about when I first came to Knoxville. There was this guy who'd stop by at least several times a week, asking if I was menstruating. That's all he'd ask, 'Are you menstruating?' 'Course I told him no every time he asked that. First I thought he was one of these guys liked to do it when the woman was bleeding. Then I got curious, so one night, after he asked me that, I say, 'Why you asking me that, man? What's your reason?' And you know what he told me? He said he was a vampire, trying to stay straight, trying to get by without having to kill somebody for their blood."

"You're not serious," Robin said.

"Honey, I'm as serious as a heart attack," the prostitute said. "He told me he robbed blood banks, did prostitutes during their menses - that's his word - things like that." She stopped, considering. "He

looked like a vampire, too," she said. "Pale-looking, weird-acting."
She shook her head. "I never let him do me, though. I got more sense
than that."

Jack shook his head disgustedly.

"So, you watch while they did the strip search?" the prostitute
asked him.

Jack looked back up. "No," he answered. "Should I have?"

"Might have made you feel better," she said, then added, "No
hard feelings, though. Judging from the look on your face, I take it
you didn't get what you were looking for."

Jack kept mute.

"You ever decide what you're gonna charge me with?" she asked.

Jack glanced at Robin. "The charge is solicitation, Ms. Doe," he
said, then got up. "I'll let Robin here handle the processing. I've got
other things I need to see to," and left.

Jack had just pulled away from the wall beside her outer door,
preparatory to heading toward the bank of elevators at the end of the
hall, frustrated and angry with her tardiness, when a ding told him an
elevator was in the process of stopping. He stopped, stood there,
staring, waiting to see if it was her. It was.

Her face brightened considerably when she saw him and she came
excitedly toward him. For a moment his anger wavered in the face of
her happiness at seeing him, but only for a moment.

Gillian came up to him, kissed him hungrily on the mouth. He
didn't respond, scowling at her when she pulled back.

"What?" she asked, innocently.

"You got any idea what time it is?" he raved at her.

She glanced at her watch, then gave him a contrite look. "Oh,
Jack, I'm sorry," she said, "some of us went out for drinks after
court, and I guess time just got away from me."

She gave him a smile, shrugged her shoulders as if speaking, what
can I say, then stepped around him and unlocked her door.

He followed her into the apartment, shutting it louder than
necessary.

She ignored that, going into the living room, throwing her trench
coat on the couch, setting her large satchel down, then sitting down
on the sofa, pulling her boots off.

"Damnit, Gillian, I've been calling all night to tell you I'd be late and been outside waiting on you for over an hour!" he fumed. "It's two o'clock in the morning, where the hell were you?"

She frowned slightly, then said, "I said I was sorry, Jack. It won't happen again."

"Again? This has become a pattern, so what makes you think it's not going to happen again?" he angrily demanded.

She studied him a moment, then, "You're mad."

He sighed heavily. "Listen, Gillian, I just think when we agree to meet at a certain time and place, you should be there. I've got better things to do with my time than stand around waiting on you to show up!" He didn't mention his frustration that she still hadn't given him a key to her apartment, even though he had given her one to his, her explanation being she liked her privacy and space. *Well, who didn't?* he had asked himself countless times.

"I don't think it would hurt you to try to be a little more responsible!" he continued.

She stood up, then approached him.

"You're right," she said, simply.

He felt his anger dissipating.

"I've acted badly," she said, almost shyly, her voice sounding little-girlish.

He didn't know how to respond to that.

She pulled her heavy sweater over her head, then undid her skirt, let it drop, stepped out of it, stood before him clad only in white, cotton panties cut high, a sleeveless t-shirt that reminded him of the one his kid sister used to wear when they were small, and heavy cotton socks. His eyes traveled over the shirt, taking note she was braless beneath. He noticed his crotch felt tighter.

"And I should be punished for my irresponsible behavior," she continued, coming closer.

He wasn't sure if he had heard her right.

"Take me into the bedroom, Jack," she whispered, standing near him.

He looked at her. Her eyes had changed, were brighter now. Her voice was different, deeper, huskier.

"Come on, Gillian, stop it," he said, feeling uncomfortable.

She stepped right up against him, looked into his eyes. "Take me into the bedroom," she whispered. "Please, Jack. Let me make it up to you."

He stood there, staring at her.

She turned, went toward the bedroom, stood at the door, watching him, then cocking her head, smiling shyly at him.

"Please," she whispered, now sounding like a little girl again.

He moaned slightly, then went toward her. She held her hand out to him. He took it. She smiled, let him lead her into the bedroom.

CHAPTER 24

At eight the next morning, Jack was awakened by the monotonous sound of his beeper going off. He groaned, raised up, realizing he was still at Gillian's, who was in the shower, judging by the sounds coming from the bathroom. He picked the beeper up off the nightstand, studied it, saw the emergency display Marvin used, cursed silently, got up, got dressed, and left, leaving his love a note.

An hour later, Bogie, Jack, Robin, and Marvin stood studying the dead man on the bed.

"Same MO, just like all the others," Marvin said, his voice low, barely above a whisper. "Hell, man, they all even look alike."

"All white men look alike to you," Jack said, his voice mild.

"This guy's younger than the others," Bogie observed, studying the body.

"Hung better," Robin observed.

"Well, this one is a bit different," Bogie said. "As per the silk scarf around the neck," he finished, waving his hand toward the corpse.

"Must have been doing that sex asphyxiation thing," Marvin said, glancing at Jack.

"That's not how he died, is it?" Jack asked, "by asphyxiation?"

"We'll let the ME confirm, but I think the fact that he's got a hole in his heart would negate that one," Bogie said.

"Shit, this is one kinky killer, I got to tell you," Marvin said, walking around the room.

"Perverted's more like it," Robin answered.

"Hell, you'd think one of them suckers would have fought back," Marvin said.

"Guess none of them saw it coming," Jack answered.

"I told you-all before," Robin said, "it's so obvious. She/he, whoever our killer is, is on top, riding him, he climaxes, she pulls out whatever the hell she's using to kill them with, wherever she hides it, slams it into his heart, and bang, the heart stops, the guy's dead before he even thinks about reacting."

Jack turned to Robin. "Where's our Jane Doe been all night?" he

160

asked.

Robin frowned. "Where we left her, in lockup. McKinley said we could keep here there for twenty-four hours, which she wasn't too happy with, believe me."

"Any idea how long this guy's been dead, Bogie?" Jack asked.

"Judging by the way the blood settled, I'd say no more than twelve, maybe fourteen hours."

They all looked at each other. "What time'd you and Tom surveile her?" Jack asked Robin.

She thought. "Seven, maybe seven-thirty."

"We got there around nine," Jack said.

"She had time," Marvin interjected.

"Yeah, but she doesn't feel right," Robin opined.

"We need to wait on the autopsy to get the true time of death," Bogie advised, "then go from there."

Marvin and Robin nodded their heads in agreement.

"You're right," Jack said. "We don't want to rush this." He went to the window, turned and glanced at the nude body on the bed, then looked around. "Okay, what's happening?" he asked.

Robin glanced up. "We've cordoned off the hotel. No one comes in or out till we've interviewed all patrons and employees."

"You got anything yet?"

"So far, zilch."

"No eye-witnesses?"

"Nada."

"What about auditory?"

"Only thing so far is the couple next door said they heard loud classical music."

Jack leaned against the window sill, staring at the deceased, then, "Anybody ID him yet?"

Marvin shook his head. "Registered as John Wayne. Again. No license, billfold, nothing on him."

"Want to bet this guy's a lawyer?" Jack asked, causing the others to laugh.

He ambled back over to the doorway, leaned against the jamb, watching the evidence technicians bagging their collections. Shit, he couldn't keep his mind on what he was doing here. He couldn't get the time he had spent with Gillian out of his head, what they had done when they went into the bedroom. How she had atoned to him for her irresponsibility. He thought he had seen it all, done it all, till Gillian had come into his life and changed that perspective. Then wondered how she would feel about him today.

"Beep me if you need me," he said, straightening up suddenly, going toward the door, ignoring everyone's raised eyebrows.

Jack went to the courthouse, found her where he knew she would be, in Chancery Court, division three, sitting at her machine, taking down a heated verbal exchange between two lawyers. He stood in the back, watching her. *God, she's so gorgeous,* he thought. Copper-colored hair, green eyes, a cat's face. Feline body: small, sleek, compact, bursting with energy, and about as mysterious as a cat. Never talking about her past except to tell him her father had been a lawyer turned judge, that both her parents were dead, and that she had no siblings. Had moved around a lot, just experiencing life, before finally deciding to settle here. "You can always find a job if you're a court reporter," she had told him with a smile on her face.

She glanced up as if she sensed him, gave him one of her shy smiles, then looked away quickly. He felt his gut twist. Man, this woman was an enigma to him; he never knew what to expect from her. Last night, she had seemed like an animal in bed and today was acting timid as a child.

He waited until the judge called recess, then stepped outside, knowing she would come to him.

She wouldn't look at him as she walked toward him, holding her face down, self-consciously playing with a stray lock of her hair, which she had pulled back into a low ponytail at the nape of her neck. He watched her come, then her taut, upturned buttocks flashed into his mind. He blinked, shook his head slightly, mumbled, "Shit" to himself.

She reached him, then boldly looked him in the eyes. He smiled, reached out, touched her face. She smiled back, as if in relief.

"So, how are you doing, Gil?" he asked her, his voice low.

"Fine. Fantastic." She closed her eyes, and when she opened them, he noticed they were dark now, as they appeared when she was passionate.

"About last night," he said, feeling like an awkward teenager, clearing his throat. "I didn't hurt you, did I?" he asked.

She looked confused for a moment, as if she wasn't sure what he meant, then smiled widely. She stepped closer to him. "You'd never hurt me deliberately, Jack, I know that. I trust you explicitly."

He sighed heavily. "I don't know, Gil. What happened was a little too extreme, I think."

She seemed to not understand him at first, then shook her head. "Jack, I know you, and you would have stopped if you thought you were hurting me or I would have asked you to. And I didn't, did I?"

She was right about that. She reached out, took his hand, led him to the alcove for the bathrooms, to a corner by themselves. "Don't fret over something that don't need fretting over," she said, her voice sounding redneck. He grinned. "What two consenting adults do behind closed doors is no one's business but theirs, right? We are adults, are we not?" He grinned again. "Consenting? Pleasuring each other?"

"Definitely," he replied.

"Well, then, who's to say what we did wasn't the right thing to do, for us."

He realized he was becoming aroused, just thinking about it, but didn't reply.

"Well, I've got to get back before they come hunting for me," she said, a little hurriedly, kissed him chastely, then headed off.

"Hey, Gil," he called after her.

She turned, smiled widely.

"See you tonight?" he asked.

"You can count on it," she said, cocking her head, grinning widely, blew him a kiss, turned and was gone.

CHAPTER 25

When Jack got back to the station, the meeting of protocol had already started. He slipped through the door and sat down, ignoring the frustrated look Marvin was giving him.

McKinley looked at him. "We got an ID on this one pretty quick, only because one of the techs down at the morgue knew him."

Jack nodded his head.

McKinley looked at his notes. "Our victim is one Mr. Carlton Bauer, Attorney at Law. His specialty is, or shall I say was, criminal defense." He grinned at the grumbling from the others over this information.

"Was the dude married?" Marvin asked.

"Yep." He looked at Marvin, then Jack. "No one's been to see the widow yet," he said.

Jack looked at Marvin. "Let's go," he said.

The house occupied by the former Carlton Bauer was located on the outskirts of Knoxville, in a small community called Powell which was the current hot spot for living and building. Jack and Marvin drove slowly through the subdivision, admiring the looming houses, neatly-groomed yards, brick-enclosed mailboxes, no telephone or electrical lines above ground, giving the cluster of homes a clean effect.

"Whatchoo think, man, half-a-mil and up?" Marvin asked, glancing at Jack.

"At least," Jack said, studying the numbers painted on the curb, looking for 1204.

He turned into a driveway ending at a three-story house, all brick and windows. After he stopped the car, Jack and Marvin sat admiring the view in front of them. "This Carlton Bauer must have done pretty well for himself," Jack said, catching a glimpse of a privacy enclosure around what looked to be a pool in the back yard.

"Hey, man, don't they all?" Marvin asked irritably, getting out of the car.

He stomped up the sidewalk. "Shit, it purely makes me sick the way these assholes live," he snarled.

Jack smiled.

"I ain't been to one attorney's house yet that lived like us normal folks," Marvin said.

"Who said we were the normal folks?" Jack asked, ribbing him.

Marvin ignored him, reached out, jabbed the bell.

A woman in her early 30's came to the door, peeked timidly out at them through the side window.

They held up their badges so she could see who they were.

She moved to the door and opened it, inserting herself into the opening, blocking their way in. She was tall and slender, dressed in a long, flimsy floral dress, with flats on her feet. Her hair was blond and shoulder-length, parted on the side. Her eyes were wide and blue. She looked to Jack to be the quintessential all-American girl.

"Could I help you?" she asked, her voice soft.

"Ms. Bauer?" Jack asked.

"Yes," she said, looking almost frantic.

Jack and Marvin glanced at each other.

"Ma'am, I'm afraid I may have some bad news for you," Jack said, making his voice as gentle as he could.

She stood there, waiting expectantly.

He cleared his throat. "We found a man's body this morning and we think he may be your husband. It seems one of the techs at the – well, someone knew him."

He stopped, watching her response. She just stared passively at him.

"Ma'am, I'd like to ask you to come to the morgue with us, view the body, and confirm whether that's your husband or not," Jack said, puzzled at her reaction to all this. After all, he had been expecting hysterics at most, tears at least.

"I'll just get my purse," she said, closing the door.

Jack and Marvin looked at each other.

"Now, that was not normal," Marvin said.

"What do you think's going on?" Jack asked, sotto voce. "You think maybe she already knew?"

"Or at least suspected," Marvin said, then shut up when the door opened.

Ms. Bauer sat in the back seat and was silent the entire way to the morgue. Jack kept glancing in the rear-view mirror, searching for any kind of reaction from her to the news they had imparted. She sat, twisting the strands of her purse, gazing out the window, seeming lost in her own thoughts.

She startled when Jack stopped the car and addressed her, jumping slightly, her face reddening.

She allowed them to escort her inside the building and into what Jack called the viewing room, waiting silently for the monitor to reveal whether the dead man inside was her husband or not.

"Are you all right?" Jack asked her. "We could wait a few moments if you need to – "

"I'm fine, really," she interrupted, not looking at him, gazing steadfastedly at the monitor. "I just wish they'd hurry," she mumbled, twisting the strands of her purse again.

Jack and Marvin exchanged glances.

When the dead man's face appeared on-screen, she gasped slightly, then turned away, one hand to her mouth, one clutching her purse to her chest.

Jack and Marvin gathered around her, waiting.

She finally seemed to realize they were there, then turned to Jack. "That's him, that's my husband," she said.

Jack drew back a little, thinking she sounded relieved, if anything. "All right, ma'am, thank you," he said, taking her by the elbow and steering her toward the door.

As they were going down the hall, she stopped and looked at Jack. He noticed there were still no signs of grief in her face.

"Ms. Bauer?" he asked.

"How did he, you know, die?" she asked. "Was it a heart attack, something like that?"

Jack glanced at Marvin but saw Marvin wasn't going to help with this one. "No, ma'am. I'm sorry to have to tell you, but your husband was murdered last night."

"Do you know who did it?" she asked.

"No, ma'am, I'm afraid we don't know that yet, but I assure you, we'll do everything to catch the perpetrator. I promise you that."

She nodded her head, processing that information, then gave Jack a defiant look. "Would you do something for me?" she asked him.

"If I can," he answered.

"When you catch the killer, whoever he is, tell him I'll be

eternally grateful," she said, then walked away.

Jack and Marvin were left standing, stunned expressions on their faces.

They finally got moving and caught up with her.

"Ms. Bauer, I think we need to talk," Jack said, catching her arm. She gave him a weary smile. "Yes, I would think so," she said.

They went to a break room in the building, and after they were all seated around a small, plastic table, Styrofoam cups containing limpid coffee in their hands, the woman began the interrogation by saying, "I suppose you're wondering at the way I've reacted to this news," studying her cup.

Jack said, "Well, Ms. Bauer, I have to tell you, your reaction was not what I would have thought it would be."

She nodded as if understanding. "My husband was an attorney," she said, "a very good one; cream of the crop, in fact." She focused her attention on her coffee cup. "I have come to the conclusion, gentlemen, that it takes a certain predatory, primitive individual to be a successful lawyer."

"Ain't that the truth?" Marvin mumbled.

Jack sat silently.

"I'm glad he's dead," she said, her voice low.

Jack leaned back, considering this.

"Ms. Bauer, maybe you want to talk to a lawyer about this," Marvin said.

She smiled like she thought this was amusing. "A lawyer? No, that's not necessary. Like I said, I wanted him dead, but I didn't kill him, so I don't see any need to consult with an attorney."

"You have that right," Jack said.

"Am I under arrest?" she asked, looking surprised.

"No, ma'am, but this is an investigation. Anything you say that may be damaging – "

She shook her head adamantly. "No, Mr. Daniels, I do not want to see or talk with a lawyer. I pray to God I never have to deal with an attorney again as long as I live." She shrugged. "After all, I'm innocent, I have nothing to hide from you."

Jack and Marvin were silent, considering this.

"You want to tell us the reason you feel the way you do about your husband being dead?" Jack finally asked her, glancing at

Marvin.

She thought for a moment. "Maybe if I tell you about him, you'll understand," she said.

"Tell us whatever you feel you need to," Marvin encouraged.

"When Carlton and I first married, he was just beginning law school," she began, making circular movements on the table top with her cup. "He was different then. Or perhaps just appeared that way in order to get what he wanted from me."

"Which was?" Jack asked.

"A meal ticket, someone to pay the bills while he went through law school, swimming with the other baby sharks in the pool." She hesitated, as if visualizing that picture. "I worked two jobs while he went to law school, worked my butt off. He kept telling me that after he graduated and got a job, things would be easier for me. He'd take care of me, I wouldn't have to worry about working. Ever." She sat back, sighed. "He was right on that score. I did not have to work again. Ever."

She opened her purse, pulled out a pack of cigarettes and lighter. "Do you mind?" she asked them.

They nodded simultaneously.

She tapped a cigarette out, placed it in her mouth, her hands visibly shaking, snapped the lighter, lit the cigarette, inhaled deeply, expelling the smoke with her eyes closed, appearing almost orgasmic.

Now, that is what I would call a true smoker, Jack thought, wanting one but aware his partner wouldn't approve.

"Once Carlton became an attorney, he changed," she continued, "or maybe became the true man he was. Whereas before I had always called him Carl, now that wasn't good enough. It had to be Carlton. I had to dress a certain way, look a certain way, talk a certain way." Her voice had taken on an acerbic tone. She stopped, took another drag. "And if I didn't, well, let's just say he made sure the bruises were never visible to anyone else."

"The dude beat you?" Marvin asked.

She seemed to shudder slightly. "Beat, stomped, kicked, whipped, flogged, you name it, he did it. I'm talking physically. Of course, he heaped on the emotional abuse, as well. Had a doctor he would take me to when the beatings got out of hand, one of his so-called friends, who'd fix me up, send me home, ready for the next go-round. I was a regular bantamweight to the Mike Tyson of the lawyer kingdom." She stopped, inhaled smoke again. Held up a wrist, showed them a scar running horizontally. "I tried to escape. Many times. This was the closest I came. Of course, he intervened, took me to his pal, got me fixed up, and when I was recovered, boy, did I pay." She traced the line with her index finger, almost lovingly. She glanced up at them. "I couldn't walk or sit for a week. I have never felt so much pain in my life."

Her eyes were dark, wet marbles.

"Why didn't you just leave?" Jack asked her.

"Oh, I tried that, too. I don't know if your friend told you anything about Carlton, but he's very well-known among other lawyers, doctors, certain political officials; the elite, let's call it. He found me each and every time. Even at a shelter for battered women. He always seemed to know who to contact to get me released back into his custody. He told me last time that if I ran away again, he'd kill me himself, slowly, painfully." Her eyes glinted. "Believe me, he would do it," she said, her voice hard.

"You never reported him to the police?" Jack asked.

She looked at him as if she couldn't believe he had said that.

"Domestic violence is a pretty serious offense," he offered.

"Not when your husband's law firm handles the sheriff's personal business," she hissed.

Jack drew back, surprised at this.

"So you stayed," Marvin stated.

"So, I stayed," she agreed, "praying that something would happen to him, that he would die a horrible, violent death; praying every time I heard his foot on the doorstep, heard his terrible, torturous voice, felt his vile, ugly hands and body on me. I prayed and prayed and prayed." Her voice had risen to a shrill pitch. She stopped, glanced around, then put the cigarette to her mouth again.

She ground the cigarette out, blowing smoke, then looked at them. Leaning toward them, her voice low, she asked, "Did he die an agonizing, painful death? Please tell me he did."

Jack and Marvin looked at each other. Finally Jack said, "Let's just say it wasn't easy, all right?"

She smiled as if happy at this. "Then my prayers have been

answered," she said, pulling out another cigarette.

Not able to stand it anymore, Jack pulled out his own pack. Marvin took the time to give him an irritated look, but Jack ignored that, lighting up.

After exhaling smoke, Jack said, "We need to ask you a few questions."

"Of course," she said.

"Where were you last night?" Jack asked, his voice hard, pulling open his note pad.

She nodded her head. "Ah, so, I am a suspect," she observed.

"Everyone's a suspect at this point," Marvin interjected.

"I watch TV, I read," she said, her voice mild. "I understand close family members, namely the surviving spouse, are usually the priority when it comes to suspects. It makes sense, don't you think?"

They watched her, waiting.

She shrugged slightly. "Carlton had called earlier and told me he would be late, so I did as I was expected to, I stayed at home, waiting."

"You weren't concerned when your husband didn't come home last night?" Jack asked.

"I was relieved, not concerned, praying something bad had happened to him," she answered, giving him an innocent look.

Jeez, thought Jack.

"Did he do that a lot?" Marvin asked.

"Do what?"

"Stay out all night, was that why you weren't so concerned about his not coming home?"

"Not until lately, maybe within the last month, then it's been once or twice a week, I guess, he'd say he had to work late, dinner with a client, whatever. A couple of times he didn't come home."

"And what did you think about that?" Jack asked.

"Like I told you, I was relieved. If he wasn't home, he wasn't beating on me."

Jack nodded.

"Did you suspect anything, you know, with the late nights?" Marvin asked.

She seemed to think a minute. "I suppose I was hoping he was having an affair. I hoped maybe he would fall in love with someone else, then want to leave me. Give me a divorce. Get out of my life. Leave me the fuck alone." Her voice had begun to rise. She glanced around, seeming embarrassed, then leaned toward them. "If it isn't obvious, I really hated that man. Hated him. I'm glad he's dead. I hope he's burning in hell as we speak," she spat, then sat back, looking fatigued.

Jack waited.

"Yes, I think he was having an affair," she finally said, her voice low. "There were the usual signs, the smell of perfume on his clothes, speaking on the phone in a low voice." She thought a moment. "And the beatings were less often, as if his thoughts were elsewhere." She shrugged, then gave them a belligerent look. "Maybe he was doing to her what he had done to me and, unlike me, she had some backbone and got back at him for it." She laughed harshly. "I sure hope so," she said, lighting another cigarette.

Jack leaned back, thinking about their Jane Doe who beat up on guys who beat up on her.

Marvin stepped in. "Did your husband have any unusual sexual proclivities?" he asked.

She looked at him, seeming to ponder, blowing smoke. "He liked to whip me, tie me up and flog me like a damn criminal. He liked for me to shave my body, all over," leaning toward them, raising her eyebrows. "That was a new one, just recent in fact."

Jack straightened up at that.

"He liked anal intercourse," she continued. "S&M, B&D. He was one bad mother fucker, gentlemen, and he deserved to die."

Jack ground out the cigarette he had been smoking, pulled out another one, lit it, ignoring Marvin's frustrated look. He sat silently for a while, watching her, processing what she had told him, searching for any sign of guilt on her part. Finally, he said, "What about enemies that you're aware of, anyone who might have wanted your husband dead?"

"Besides you, of course," Marvin said.

She thought, her eyes studying the wall behind them. She finally shrugged, said, "Carlton didn't have any friends that I'm aware of other than whoever he had been seeing recently. As for enemies, I'd say he had plenty. Do you know what his partners called him? The pit-bull of the law firm. He was mean, gentlemen, evil. He could take one look at you and before you knew it, recognize what your weakness was. He had a talent for that. Then he'd go for the jugular, bring you to your knees, if that was what he wanted to do. So, yes, I'd say Carlton had many enemies."

Damn, Jack thought, glancing at Marvin.

"This person you suspected he was seeing," Marvin said, "he never gave you any indication who it might have been? Maybe a secretary, someone with the firm?"

"No, he never told and I knew better than to ask," she answered tersely.

She startled them by putting her hands over her face and beginning to weep. They looked at each other, then at her, not sure what to do, then sat there uncomfortably until she was finished. She finally drew her hands away, dug in her purse, came up with a tissue, wiped her eyes, then blew her nose. She glanced embarrassedly at them. "I'm sorry, I'm just so relieved," she said, dabbing her nose. "I know this probably makes me suspect to you, but I just can't help it," then began crying again.

After she had gotten herself under control, Jack and Marvin decided to take her home, advising her as they walked her to her front door that they would be in touch if they had any further questions and not to leave the area until further notice.

Once they were inside the car, they looked at each other.

"Well, what do you think?" Marvin asked.

"I don't know, man, but I'm inclined to think she didn't do it," Jack answered, starting the car. "Lord knows, she had cause, but I can't see her having the nerve to go after him like that."

"Especially in a hotel room," Marvin said. "I mean, if she was gonna off the guy, why not just do it there at home? Claim the battered wife syndrome, show her bruises?"

Jack nodded, then said, "Unless, of course, that's what she wants us to think."

They looked at each other.

"Then again we got our prostitute with the violent propensity."

"Yeah, boy. What was it she said, they beat on her, she beats back harder?" Marvin agreed. "But the window's awful slim there, guy."

"We'll know for sure once the autopsy's done," Jack said, backing out of the driveway.

"'Course, there's always Oberman," Marvin sighed.

CHAPTER 26

He had been sitting hunched down in an unmarked sedan across the street from the parking lot to Gillian's apartment complex, watching, waiting, wondering. Night had fallen and it was misting slightly. Everything seemed to be cast in gray, he didn't know from his depression or from the weather. He didn't care.

Jack glanced at his watch. They had a date planned an hour from now. Her car was in the lot, but he didn't want to go in, not yet. He knew he should be at the station, waiting on the autopsy report, but he found himself here instead. *God, I'm tired*, he thought, rubbing his face roughly with his hands. He glanced toward Gillian's car. Even though she had promised time after time to be more vigilant about keeping dates with him and to be where she was supposed to, she continued to mysteriously disappear. After last night, he was determined to find out where she was going.

Why can't I give this up, he wondered to himself. *Why can't I just trust her?* Gut instinct, he knew, was his motivation here. But why? What was he sensing subconsciously he wouldn't acknowledge?

What was she so secretive about? Did he really want to know? Did he want to face whatever consequences lay ahead if he kept this surveillance up? *Yes*, he told himself. Simply because it had become harder and harder to keep his mind focused on his job, on tracking their killer, while all the time wondering where Gillian was and what she was doing. Jack had decided that until he found out what his lover was so guarded about, he would not be able to fully concentrate on finding the person committing all these killings. So here he sat.

He closed his eyes, lay his head against the back of the seat, feeling weary. He wasn't sure if he dozed or just blanked out for a few seconds, but when he opened his eyes, there her car was, pulling out of the parking lot, heading away from him. He couldn't see who was driving.

Shit, he thought, starting his car, making a U-turn, trying to catch up to her but appear as if he wasn't.

He made it a point to stay two to three car lengths behind her, always keeping another vehicle between them, not allowing himself to speculate where she may be headed.

She drove to a motel in North Knoxville. Jack turned into the lot, pulling off to the side, watching where her car went. After it disappeared around the side of the three-story, rectangular building, he followed. As he came around the back, she was pulling into a space near the stairway. He pulled to the farthest corner of the parking lot, underneath a tall Maple tree, beyond the clutching fingers of light shed by a security lamp, watched as she exited her car, wearing a trench coat and carrying her satchel. Her hair looked dark, but he figured that was due to the night and reflection of the halogen lights glowing yellow.

As Gillian went up the outside staircase, he wondered what she was doing with her satchel, wondered if she was there to take a deposition, but that late in the evening? He watched as she went up the stairs to the second floor, turned right, then walked down the open balcony, checking room numbers.

When she came to room 207, Gillian stopped, knocked, stood waiting. A man came to the door, smiling when he saw her, opening the door wider, reaching out, pulling her to him as he closed the door. Jack recognized this man as the one Gillian had been with that night, when she blew him off, acting so strange.

Jack felt his pressure go up 100 points. *What the hell is she doing with this guy?* he wondered to himself. *I thought she said it was nothing, he didn't mean anything to her, she was using him.*

Jack sat there seething, trying to gain control of his temper. He finally got out of his car, went to the stairs, practically ran up them, approached room 207, walked past, to the end of the hall, then turned back.

He paced back and forth, trying to fight the maddening impulse to ram the door down, stop them right in the middle of whatever the fuck they were doing. *Right,* he thought disgustedly to himself. *That's exactly what they're doing.*

He stood outside the door, his hands clenched, his face red. His attention was distracted when he heard voices and the sound of a man and a woman on the stairs.

He put his head down, walked toward the stairs, seeming to be a man in a hurry, got on, went down to the parking lot, noticed a restaurant and bar to the left of the stairs on the ground floor.

Jack decided he'd wait there until she came down, approach her, find out what the hell was going on with her, once and for all. He couldn't stand it anymore, the secretiveness, her guardedness, the never being where she was supposed to be, never being on time, always putting his questions off or giving vague explanations.

Jack went inside, took a seat in a booth by the window, ordered a beer, sat there brooding, watching the stairway. He couldn't help but speculate what was going on behind that closed door upstairs. The thought of Gillian with another man, of what he could be doing to her, her to him, was driving him insane. He kept getting up, going toward the exit, but would stop himself, restlessly returning to his seat, drinking more beer.

Jack knew he should try to control the alcohol, knew he could get to the point where what was rational to him in a more stable frame of mind wouldn't be, but he wanted to dull the images his brain was perceiving, dull his senses, deaden his emotions.

Jack waited for over an hour. He had consumed three beers by then. Instead of mottling his feelings, the alcohol only seemed to escalate them. His anger was like hot steam coursing through his blood. He could feel his face burn, his fingers tingled, his fists clenched and unclenched.

Finally, he couldn't wait anymore. He had to know. He decided he would risk everything, barge down the door if he had to, confront her, get this out in the open, deal with it here, now. Kill the man and her, if they were doing what he suspected.

He stalked out the door, went to the stairs, started up. An elderly couple stepped on behind him. Jack turned, pulled out his badge, said, "This is police business, get out of here," and waited impatiently as they hustled off.

He was up the stairs in a flash, his anger propelling him down the outer hallway, and without thinking what he was doing, without even hesitating, he pulled his leg back, bashed the door beside the knob with his foot, did it once, twice, three times, and then stood there when the door swung open, holding his hand out to catch it as it swung back, and stepped inside.

The rich, coppery smell was incredible, clinging to the air like dew on grass. He fought the urge to gag, moving from the entryway into the main room, then toward the bedroom, thinking, *Oh, God, let*

Gillian be all right, please don't let anything have happened to Gillian.

He pushed the door open to the bedroom and what he saw brought him to his knees. He stayed there, swaying slightly, his mind refusing to register what he was witnessing.

His lover was standing on the bed nude, wearing a black wig, obscenely straddling the man's head on the pillow beneath her, writing something on the wall behind the bed in large red letters, stopping after each one to stoop and dip the object she was writing with in the blood from the genital area of the man sprawled naked on the bed. She was so intent on what she was doing, she hadn't even heard his forced entry into the suite, nor his harsh keening as he now watched her in shocked awareness.

"Sweet Mother of God," Jack moaned, but she ignored him, continuing at her labor.

He forced himself to stand, stood there, fighting the urge to vomit, tears running down his face. "My God, Gillian, what have you done?" he finally said, his voice low, raw.

She stopped immediately, then turned to face him. Her face was rigid, set in stone.

She stared at him a moment, then hissed, "My name's Ronnie, not Gillian," and went back to her letters.

EPILOGUE
THREE MONTHS LATER

Jack was sitting in the back of the courtroom, waiting for Gillian's case to be called before the court, when Marvin sat down beside him.

"Hey, bro," Marvin said, grinning widely at him.

Jack nodded his head, then turned his attention to the front of the courtroom.

"Sarge said he needs you back, Jack," Marvin said, his voice sobering.

Jack glanced at him.

"What are you gonna do, man, beat yourself up forever over this case?" Marvin asked, exasperatedly.

Jack turned to him. "I should have known. I should have figured it out. The signs were there, I just didn't pick up on them."

"You're full of shit if that's what you're thinking," Marvin said. "Hell man, your girlfriend not keeping dates isn't any reason to suspect she's a serial killer."

Jack stayed silent.

"You talked to her?" Marvin asked.

"Her lawyer says she wants to see me, I don't know." Jack mumbled.

"That might be what you need to do, you know, talk to her," Marvin said. "Maybe then you can forgive yourself for loving the wrong woman."

Jack turned back to him. "Thanks for coming that night, partner. Thanks for getting me out of there. I don't think I could have handled having to arrest her. I know I was nuts by the time you got there."

"I think we were all nuts that night, man." Marvin shook his head. "It was weird, Jack. She kept claiming she was this Ronnie till we had her at the station, then she said she was Gillian and didn't understand why we had her there."

"Her attorney says she still doesn't understand it," Jack said.

"She pleading insanity?" Marvin asked.

"I don't know. That or MPD, I guess."

178

"You think that will fly?" Marvin asked.

"Hell if I know," Jack said.

"You think it's true? You think she actually has, what's it called, an alternate personality?" Marvin asked.

Jack looked at him. "You saw her, you talked to her, what do you think?"

Marvin sat back. "Yeah, man, I think she does. She was like two entirely different people that night, weirdest thing I ever saw."

Jack nodded his head.

"So, you coming back to the force or not?" Marvin asked.

"I don't know," Jack said. "I need some time, Marvin, I need to get some things straight in my head."

"You're copping out's what you're doing," Marvin said, getting up. "Listen, man, I got to go. Call me, Jack. I ain't gonna let you get off the hook this easy, you hear?"

Jack glanced up and away. "Sure," he said, his attention on the front of the courtroom.

A few minutes later, a bailiff approached him and told him Ms. McKenzie's attorney would like to speak to him in the hall outside the courtroom.

Jack stepped outside and went to meet one of the best criminal defense attorneys Knoxville had to offer, someone he knew had been a friend of Gillian's, before.

"Herschel," Jack said, shaking hands, wondering why Gillian or Ronnie had passed on this guy, who seemed to meet her protocol, then thinking maybe she knew she might need him someday.

The attorney led him to an alcove.

"Court's been delayed for an hour or so, the judge is hearing a motion in chambers on another case. Gillian wants to talk to you, Jack. She asked me to see if you'd be willing to visit with her for a minute."

Jack hesitated.

"She's innocent, you know," Herschel went on. "She's truly sick, Jack. I want you to remember that. The person who killed those people isn't the person you loved."

Jack nodded his head, looking away, then back. "Okay," he said.

Herschel led Jack to a small anteroom, opening the door for him, then closing it behind him. Jack stood right inside the door, looking at Gillian, who was seated near the window. Her hands were handcuffed. A female officer stood near her.

"Jack," Gillian said, her voice cracking. "I'm so glad you came," she added, tears rolling down her face.

He approached her as she stood, then accepted her hug, not returning it. She clung to him fiercely for a moment, then sensing his uneasiness, stepped back from him.

"They've told me the terrible things that happened," she said, looking at him. "Jack, please believe me, I didn't know she was doing it, I didn't know it was happening. I mean, I knew I was sick, I knew there was something wrong with me, I just . . ." She stopped, then, "I never would have thought any part of me would be capable of that," she said, then sat down heavily, put her face in her hands.

Jack pulled a chair out, sat down next to her.

She finally stopped crying, looked at him. "I'm sorry I hurt you. I'm sorry for what I put you through," she said.

Jack felt his heart lift a bit but wouldn't allow himself to speak.

"Herschel says I need psychiatric help," she added, then smiled slightly. "Well, duh," she added, trying for levity. She stopped smiling. "They're going to put me in a psychiatric hospital, Jack. The DA's office has worked out some kind of deal with Herschel. They ran all these tests on me, all kinds of psychiatrists and psychologists have talked to me, and everyone seems to think it would be best if I just go away, I guess. Apparently, I've become some sort of precedent case and the DA's afraid of opening up a huge can of worms if I'm found innocent." She stopped talking, looking at him.

"I always loved looking at your beautiful face," she said, her voice soft. "I'll always love you, Jack, I want you to know that, I'll always hold you dear to my heart, but I don't think I'll be leaving where they're sending me, not for a long time anyway. And I wanted to see you just to tell you how I feel and how deeply sorry I am for what I've done to you."

He reached out, took her hands in his.

"You're a wonderful man, Jack," she whispered. "You made me stronger. I almost overcame her, through you. Almost." She pulled her hands away, wiping her face.

"Gillian – "

"No, don't say anything," she said, her voice stronger. "I

understand. I think the best thing you can do for me and for you is to forget me, Jack. Let me go. Understand that there wasn't anything you could do to stop me and now there's nothing you can do to help me." She leaned toward him. "Go back to the police department, Jack, don't give that up. You're too good at what you do. They need you."

He looked sharply at her.

She smiled at him. "Robin comes to see me occasionally. She tells me what's going on. She's really a nice woman. I like her a lot. She's your friend, Jack, she can help you." She glanced at the guard, then turned back to him. "If you don't mind, Jack, I'd like you to leave now. This is hard for me and I'm getting tired. I'd like to rest before I have to go into the courtroom."

He nodded his head, stood, wanting to say so many things to her, not trusting himself to say them in the right way. She sat with her head cast down, not watching him.

He turned, walked to the door.

"Jack," she called after him.

He turned, looked at her. Her face had changed, become harder, her eyes were brighter, her voice harsher.

"I had such fun playing with you, Jack," she said.

"Goodbye, Ronnie," he said.

Her laughter trailed him out of the room.

~ The End ~

Printed in the United States
809700001B

9 7